C000006778

Praise for Marlene

Agaat

I was immediately mesmerized ... Van Niekerk's achievement is as
brilliant as it is haunting. – Toni Morrison

Narrative creation of the highest order. – Patrick Denman Flanery,
Times Literary Supplement

Books like *Agaat* ... are the reason people read novels, and the reason
authors write them. – Liesl Schillinger, *The New York Times*

Van Niekerk has created a work of stunning breadth and emotional
potency ... an unforgettable reading experience that transcends the lives
of its four primary characters to implicate the broader world.
– Gwendolyn Dawson, *Publishing Perspectives*

Van Niekerk's novel is an intimate yet radical engagement with
Afrikaner culture that is at the same time a major contribution
to the world's literature. – Derek Attridge

Few books I've read carry the visceral impact of Marlene van Niekerk's
Agaat ... it is stunning. – Mary Gaitskill, *Bookforum*, 2010

Triomf

An astonishing departure for Afrikaans literature ... this is an
extraordinary novel and a milestone for South African literature.
Those who thought, as I did, that white writing would run out of road
in post-apartheid South Africa could not have been more wrong.
– Justin Cartwright, *Daily Telegraph*

South Africa's only world-class tragicomic novel, the kind of book that stabs at your heart while it has you rolling on the floor ... Van Niekerk's greatest fictional gifts are theatrical: her impeccable ear and her ability to bring to life a family that never stops creating scenes.
– Rob Nixon, *The New York Times*

A tempestuous, heartbreaking, exhilarating read.
– Elisabeth Vincentelli, *Time Out New York*

The tenderness of the writing, eliciting an unexpected compassion in the reader, is remarkable in a first-time novelist. It is not hard to poke fun at Afrikaners: to reveal their underlying humanity is a much more impressive accomplishment. – David Robson, *The Sunday Telegraph*

Van Niekerk's extraordinary novel ... offers a devastating glimpse of an under-class locked into a cycle of poverty and despair.
– Christina Patterson, *The Observer*

This superb translation of *Triomf* delivers a shot of adrenalin to the South African English novel ... Van Niekerk offers a realistic story of stunning complexity and a post-modernist allegory: a novel of ideas.
– Eve Bertelsen, *The Sunday Independent*

For taking us beyond ... indignant images of the despised and dejected, Van Niekerk and her translator, Leon de Kock, deserve the richest accolades. In some senses, the post-apartheid novel, free at last of political guilt and weightiness, begins right here.
– Guy Willoughby, *The Sunday Times*

Widely considered the outstanding Afrikaans novel of the 1990s ... *Triomf* is exquisitely written. – *The Economist*

The Snow Sleeper

Translated by Marius Swart

Marlene van Niekerk

Human & Rousseau

First published in Dutch in 2009 as *De Sneeuwslaper* by Querido
First published in Afrikaans in 2010 as *Die sneeuslaper* by Human & Rousseau

First published in 2019 by Human & Rousseau,
an imprint of NB Publishers,
a division of Media24 Boeke (Pty) Ltd,
40 Heerengracht, Cape Town 8001
www.humanrousseau.com

Painting on cover:
The Death of the Author, 2003, oil on canvas, 40 cm x 50 cm
by Marlene Dumas
Cover design by Keith Dietrich

Originally printed in South Africa
ISBN: 978-0-7981-7903-4 (First edition, first impression 2019)

LSiPOD: 978-0-7981-7925-6 (Second edition, first impression 2019)

ISBN 978-0-7981-7904-1 (epub)
ISBN 978-0-7981-7905-8 (mobi)

A writer is someone who spends years patiently trying to discover the second being inside him.
– Orhan Pamuk, from *My Father's Suitcase*

Contents

The Swan Whisperer

An Inaugural[i] Lecture

Honourable Rector, Dean, dear colleagues, friends and family,

What does one teach, when one is a teacher of Creative Writing? Is one concerned with the true, the good, the beautiful? With criticism or fantasy or faith? What is the use of literature, its place on the greater canvas of human endeavour? And maybe I should ask: Can a story offer consolation?

I do not pretend to have answers. What I want to share with you tonight is an experience which made this kind of question irrelevant to me. It concerns a correspondence I had with a student – I shall call him Kasper Olwagen – or rather one he had with me, as I never engaged.

Perhaps, I thought, this whole episode would become clearer to me if I reconstructed the sequence of my student's unusual letters and my reactions to them; even more so if I did this before a critical audience.

The sand is running through the hourglass; judge for yourselves. I present the evidence.

The first piece to arrive in my postbox from Kasper was a letter, if you can call it that. Sixty-seven pages. Let me read you the first paragraphs, to give you an idea of what I was dealing with.

Bed B
Ward 1002
Intensive Care Unit
Academisch Medisch Centrum
Amsterdam

24 February 2002

Dear Professor Van Niekerk

As you can deduce from the address, I am writing to you in a state of personal crisis. Ruled paper, leaking ballpoint, IV in the back of my hand, catheter in my anther. I know that a letter like this is the last thing you would expect from me, after all those years of reading my bone-dry manuscripts. I also know you prefer to keep your students at a distance, given that you are constantly having to read their boring and barely veiled confessions. Not that you ever had reason to fear anything like that from me, in all my years of study. But the time of reckoning (tempus fugit!) has come. I know you well enough to know that what I have to say will not bore you. But as you always say, no desire without technique, every truth needs an orator. And so I shall keep in mind – as much as this genre of spontaneous communication called a "letter" allows – the admonishments inked onto my manuscripts in your barbed hand. Cut to the chase, Kasper! Shorter sentences, Olwagen! Suggestion, not interpretation! Stick to the knitting, orientate your reader in space and time! Lie, but do not deceive!

Against this last, an accusation of fraud, I wish to defend myself in advance. Despite having woken only three days ago from what the nursing staff here refer to as a "babbling delirium", and while still being held in the intensive care unit for observation, I have concrete evidence that I have not dreamt up what had occurred. I am in possession of the coat, the shoes, perhaps the tongue of someone else, but let me not mislead you. I assure you I have no energy to fabricate tall tales right now. Frankly, if my tribulations in Amsterdam have had any impact, it has been to cure me finally of my ambition to write fiction. So herewith I give notice: I am dropping out of the course. Sorry for wasting your precious time. But may I suggest you regard this letter as a form of compensation? I would not be surprised if you exploit what I relate here for one of your dark designs.

*

Kasper Olwagen – as I am calling him – was thirty years old at the time of writing this letter, already a philosophy graduate. A slight, pale fellow with intense eyes, a high forehead, a delicate mouth. Well groomed, especially his hands, a skin sensitive to sun and cold. His movements seemed somewhat tentative, and his nostrils twitched constantly, as though inspecting the air for the faintest of hints. He gave an impression of fragility. His classmates nicknamed him Mr Xenos. He was intelligent, obsessive, withdrawn, a bookworm who lisped slightly when he was nervous or excited. There was something old-fashioned about his manner. For appointments he wore a waistcoat, a ruby-red bow tie, a fountain pen in the inner pocket of his jacket. I remember how he would take it out to make notes in his small black notebook, hesitantly, as though he wanted first to touch his heart.

On my recommendation, Mr Xenos was spending three months overseas during the local summer recess of 2001/2002. By chance, I had heard of a bursary available to a young, unpublished writer from South Africa – funding and accommodation at the Stichting Literaire Activiteiten Moederstad, the "mother city" being Amsterdam. I thought it would be ideal for this candidate. Exposure to a stimulating environment, as well as pressure from his Dutch hosts to produce something. Pressure from me, at any rate, had turned out to be completely counterproductive. He was one of those students, you see, who simply could not finish his writing project for the MA course, hindered as he was by extended writer's block. I guessed it was a matter of oversensitivity to criticism, alienation from his peers, confusion about the South African reality, perfectionism, hypochondria. He suffered from what he called a "murmuring heart" – suppressed libido, I suspected at the time. But after what happened to him, my projections seem misplaced. Something quite beyond my comprehension was troubling him.

On the day I received the letter, I read only the first two paragraphs and then put it aside. I was writing fiction myself at that point, in the home stretch of a novel, final revisions, surrounded by the usual chaos of that part of the process – frozen meals from Nice 'n Easy, dirty dishes, a mouse in the kitchen, squirrels in the attic, garden overgrown, wrist inflamed from using the other kind of mouse; I simply saw no sense in spending more time on a difficult student who wanted to drop out. Why didn't I try to convince him to reconsider? Well, I was tired of struggling with Kasper Olwagen. In the five years since enrolling, he had handed work in late every time, pieces riddled with too much detail, full of information and illustration, in which absolutely nothing ever happened. "Instruction manual!" I always commented. "Delete unnecessary details." His other problem was profundity. He often discussed the central question of ethics: What is a good person, how should a good person live? But always in the form of wholly indigestible allegories. Beside each and every one of his moralistic figures I wrote in the margin, "Delete the ideas." He simply could not arrive at a narrative reconciliation of meaning and minutiae. Kasper Olwagen is a philosopher, not a writer, that is what I thought.

But here was this letter from Amsterdam, quivering with appetisers from the very first paragraph. Why did I not read further? Well, I was busy. I dropped a card in the post: "Speedy recovery, thanks for your entertaining letter, I shall notify University Administration. Best."

Two weeks later, the letter resurfaced from beneath a stack of papers and I thought to myself, let's keep this on file, just in case. As I was punching holes in it, the following paragraph caught my eye. I was irritated; I find such impertinence unacceptable in a student. Just listen to this:

Professor, I still do not understand everything that has happened to me in this city; in fact, it is still happening. I am dumbfounded as I lie here in my hospital bed, and I believe that you will be similarly dumbfounded once you reach the end of this letter, even though you are employed at an institution of higher learning where space no longer exists for being dumbfounded, for fear and fascination, for grace and awe as human potentialities. I am returning to South Africa in a month's time. To whom else could I possibly confess this premonition of my fate? As you know, I am a loner. Loner! How dubious, this concept. Nobody is truly alone; an invisible string connects us all, and it is only a matter of time before we stand face to face, asking: Have we not met somewhere before? Granted, my relationship with you is by no means an example of this, Professor. But may I say that, despite all your prescriptiveness and indifference, I have always experienced you as a kind of mother, although you are not exactly brimming with the milk of human kindness? I shall leave it at that. Not all of your students feel about you the way I do, I can assure you. But let me get to the point.

Point, what point, I thought as I flicked through the pages. Three deleted pages, each line carefully struck through so that one could still read it all. So I read it, obviously. A minutely detailed description of the accommodation in Amsterdam that I had helped him obtain. Instruction manual, I thought. Here is the gist of what he had deleted.

It was a writer's paradise. Even lying here in the intensive-care unit, in the care of the Dutch nursing staff, I can recall it vividly. Will I still find it as I left it, with all my belongings, what now seems an eternity ago? An apartment on the fourth floor, close to Amsterdam harbour at the top of the Geldersekade. Three double windows with small panes in the living room. Thick, old glass, slightly discoloured, full of little bubbles and flaws. To the north, a view of the seventeenth-century gabling on the quay. To the east, the former docks, where two bright yellow cranes were constantly lifting and lowering building materials. With my binoculars (always bring your binoculars, you had said) I could make out the name Liebherr on their masts. There were two writing tables, just as you had told me to specify on the application form, one for prose against the wall, where the computer sat, and one for poetry by the window. There were two bedrooms: a small cabin on the ground floor with a view onto the back of the Sint Nicolaas church, and a larger one on the top floor. But I could not write a single word.

The usual Olwagen refrain. I impaled the letter on the levers in the file and clicked the clamp into place. After all the rattling of drums in the opening lines, nothing extraordinary; a description of a space. And dumbfounded? About what could he possibly be dumbfounded? Probably about the enormous, undeserved privilege of spending three months in such quarters for free.

And then he goes and gets himself admitted to the intensive care unit, surely not as a result of tremendum et fascinans, but rather through utter laziness. I was livid. All the forms and testimonials and special words whispered to colleagues in Amsterdam to give this student a chance, and he messes it up. I ripped Kasper Olwagen's freshly filed letter from my file and shoved it into a drawer full of speed fines, bills and final notices.

Eight months later, as I was reviewing the translation of my novel, I received notice of a package from the post office. Local, according to the slip. Could not be urgent. Kasper, I knew, had come back in the meantime; the university administration had let me know that he had deregistered in person. I wondered what had become of him, but why would I concern myself further with Mr Xenos? He had not had the decency to come and see me, to explain himself. I only fetched the package a week after the third and final notice was delivered. I remember the day I fetched it at the post office in Die Boord. My parcels, mostly from publishers, are always professionally packaged, with printed address labels. Not this one. This was wrapped up in brown paper, bound and quartered with white sisal twine, with a knob of red wax on the knot at the back. I recognised the fountain-pen script at once. I cursed. When I opened the package in the kitchen, a number of audio cassettes clattered down at my feet. Sixteen TDK cassettes, sixty minutes each. And something else – yes, nothing less than the dummy of my novel, already published by that time. I had given it to Kasper as a lucky charm on the day of his departure for Amsterdam. A handy white blank book, sturdily bound, two hundred and fifty pages, the maximum number for a novel. I had written in the front: "To Kasper, for your ideas, for the missives the gods let fall upon the streets." He looked at me strangely after reading that inscription, hand on his heart, his nostrils twitching, as though I had handed him something that smelt slightly bad.

There was a note in the parcel:

Dear Professor Van Niekerk. The heart guards its sorrow, here as in Amsterdam. I have included a few samples for you. You might find it entertaining to see what has become of your phantom book; quite fitting, I think. I call it The Logbook of a Swan Whisperer *(see my letter earlier this year from the university hospital). The contents of the tapes should amuse you even more. It means even less. All details have been deleted, all ideas have been removed. Farewell to the world of will and representation. Kind regards. Kasper.*

I kicked at the cassettes on the kitchen floor, rereading the note. Swan whisperer? What in god's name was a swan whisperer? I had heard of a horse whisperer, but a swan whisperer? Clearly, I had not read enough of Kasper's godforsaken letter.

I ripped off the rest of the brown paper, opened my model book. At least half of it was filled with writing. I had to fetch my glasses – it was written in Olwagen's characteristic fountain-pen script. Long tables, columns with headings: location, time, and action; a strict chronology of dates in the rows, 11 December 2001 to 15 January 2002. Under "Location", the entries were mostly the names of various bridges along the canal belt, and under "Action" a few cryptic notes; they looked like descriptions of some occult scheme. I have brought the book along, let me read you a few typical inscriptions: 11 December; "Prinsengracht bridge, Utrechtsestraat. Swan whisperer: posture particularly stiff today, supplication with murmuring, hands lifted, rope ladder down to the water, three swans from under the bridge". Or: "Lauriergracht bridge. Swan whisperer raises his eyes to the firmament, shakes coat out over the water, murmurs constantly, one swan from under the bridge." Invariably: bridge, gestures and swans; gestures, murmurings, swans and bridge; the same phrases over and over again.

The tapes were different, clearly from a more recent period. They were labelled from 1 to 16, with dates ranging from 5 March to 17 May 2002. I picked them up from the floor and put them into a plastic bag from Woolworths. My cassette player was broken, but I could imagine what was on them. Names of grasses, rocks, insects. Read out in alphabetical order from reference books. That is how I knew Mister Stranger.

So, this was the contents of package number two. And there I sat with my cross-dressed book and the Woolworths bag and the cut white string with the red wax in my hands. The Olwagen mock-up of my book alone was enough for me to go and open the drawer where I had shoved his letter. Drawer whisperer, I moaned, because it was so full of rubbish that it would not open.

The letter was completely scrunched up and I had to smooth it out, page by page, before I could read it.

Dear listeners, it is time now for Kasper's story. Let me orientate you once more, for clarity's sake. Imagine, if you will, a young man from the swanless south, an alien in a world city, a struggling writer, alone, anguished, neurotic. He breaks down, as is to be expected. There he lies, in a foreign hospital, his tongue feels swollen, his hands shake from the medicine they are giving him, and he writes his teacher a letter about what has supposedly happened to him. Pure fantasy? The true situation disguised? A hidden confession? An embellishment of his own failure? An attempt to mask his fears and longings? Whichever of these it may be, he hands in a logbook, a piece of evidence to support the validity of his story. Come, we shall let him set his stage:

It was, Professor, as they say over here, in the time of the dark days before Christmas. I had been eating nothing but baked beans from tins for weeks. At night I did not go to bed, but fell asleep on the red sofa in front of the television. I did not go out any more. I spent entire mornings standing at the window, rocking my head back and forth so that the quay, the docks, the traffic in the street all appeared to me in turn, variously distorted. Then I would breathe on the glass and write words on it. Guilt, penance, loss, shame. The great black bells in my tower. The reasons I could never write anything. Just once, I wrote: beauty, breath, song – and started crying.

Then I woke one morning, like a prince in the mist. A great night mist, frozen to the elms as in a fairy tale. Pure lacework in the trees alongside the quay. I blew on the windowpane and on it I wrote a line of poetry I remembered from somewhere: "Perhaps my whisper was born before my lips."

Professor, we are there to invoke, you always said, to evoke, to call forth. Why, once the lesson is manifested, is the master absent from the student's side?

Because when I erased the line with my fingertip, there he stood, framed in the trace of my breath, across the canal in a portico, a man with snow-white hair and a bag in his hand, and he stepped forward and leaned over the railing. Had he dropped something in the water? He gestured over the railing, towards the bridge arching between the canal and the harbour, his bundle beside him on the ground. I adjusted my binoculars. He was in his late forties, maybe fifty, scruffy, homeless. Tufts of down were leaking from his jacket. His lips were moving. I followed his gaze to the still water beneath the arch of the bridge. What did he see there?

He straightened, still murmuring, his hands in the air like a conductor before the orchestra strikes up. And then he gave the first beat. And from under the bridge came two swans, swimming towards him, majestic, bowing their necks, as if they belonged to him.

It was as if I saw for the first time what a swan is: feathery raiment of milk-white glass, a neck blown in a dream of fire, a vase under sail, coupled to its reflection, masked twins, breast to breast in a dance, a dark music in the webs.

The swan caller untied his bundle, and — yes, read on, it says what it says, Professor — took out a rope ladder, with which he lowered himself to the deck of a small sailboat docked at the quay.

A god in the crib of the rime-white dawn.

On his stomach, with his hands stretched out over the water, he called the birds, their tails wagging, their heads close to his. Orpheus on the bank. That I could write with my finger, in my meagre breath, one line by a forgotten poet, and have it leap from pane to quay and change into a swan whisperer ... Such serendipity enchants the heart.

*

I did not buy it. Do you? I could guess what was going to happen next. And I was right.

Kasper falls under the spell of the so-called swan whisperer — which translates as: He falls for his own fantasy about the swan whisperer, and unto us a story is born. Every day he follows him through the city, and at every bridge he bears witness to this homeless man's so-called swan ritual. The man lifts his hands like a priest, he murmurs something, a magic word or formula, the swans come from under the bridge as though summoned, and the swan master descends his rope ladder and bewhispers them.

And then follows a passage which I simply cannot neglect to read to you. My correspondent writes:

At this point I can hear your thoughts, Professor. You are thinking: This is not going to get interesting, Kasper. Your story contains: 1. A writer with writer's block. 2. A pair of binoculars. 3. A maladjusted vagrant with a swan fixation. This is not enough material, I smell a parable, you will have to get your characters involved with each other, because there is nothing like relationships between people for getting rid of symbols. I know, dear Prof, that given your limitations you will not be able to read this letter as a cry for help. You will appraise it as a piece of writing and nothing more. Well, luckily writing and living coincide entirely in this letter, because involvement is precisely what happened to me, the very next day, when I spotted the man across the way again. I went outside and followed him down the rope ladder onto the boat. What was it he smelt of? The aroma of compost? I lay down beside him on my stomach on the deck. The eager pupil. Would you not have done the same? Would you not have tried to discover what he was whispering to the swans? Could it be scripture, written on the plumb line of their flanks, runes from the cygnic depths?

With or without scripture, dear listeners, from here on the story picks up pace. Kasper takes the vagrant home, yes, Kasper feeds the vagrant. Young, unsociable South African man, an overbred neurotic afraid of germs, offers accommodation to a grimy, maladjusted stranger. And in this tale it does not stop at lodgings, it turns into nursing. Because this swan whisperer was not well. And moreover – Kasper the philosopher takes pains to impress this upon his reader – this patient of his was a blank page.

For what hero would want to take care of an eloquent invalid? Kasper's was a tight-lipped stray. The man could not or would not talk. His gaze was dull and vacant. He was purposeless and passive. He did not even know how to use the bathroom. This is how it played out:

I removed his grimy coat and the worn-out trousers and shirt. He did not have any underwear, and wore his boots without socks. I was shocked. He was very thin. There was brown gunge around his ankles and wrists and neck. His frayed clothes stuck to a crust that covered his entire body. Together with his body hair, it formed a kind of flaky silver fleece. Was this the reason for his odd odour? A layer of rotting hide? In his crotch, the hair formed a thick, caked mat. His sex was shrunken. The hair under his arms was long and white. His toenails and fingernails were overgrown and badly torn.

I put on the dishwashing gloves from the kitchen drawer and made him sit on a stool in the shower. I sponged his body down, soaped him up with disinfectant and started washing him carefully with a soft cloth.

Why did trying to clean him feel so much like trespassing? Can you explain that to me, Professor? You who understand these things so well? Why did such sorrow engulf me as I stood washing this damaged person? I was grateful for the steam, the water my tears could run into without being noticed. Who was I actually washing here? And how was I to complete what I had started? I helped him stand up, pressing my forehead against his chest to keep him upright, while using my body to prop him up as I turned him around in the shower stall.

I was scared to death, there under the shower, to strip him of his shell. But as far as I could tell, it would be more deadly not to try, deadlier for him, and even more deadly for me, do you see?

My clothes were soaked and the bathroom was completely steamed up. I caught a glimpse of our ghostly figures in the mirror, him with his hand on my shoulder, where I had put it to scrub his upper arm. Did I long for him to extend a limb or shift his weight, to give a sign of wanting to cooperate, of being willing to help me help him?

I was startled by the effect of my ablutions. Where the crust came off, his skin was tender, with inflamed red patches on the flanks and around his waist, something that looked like scabies. Or was it shingles? A proliferating eczema? Psoriasis? There were rough areas on his arms and legs, and in some places his skin seemed bruised, suffused with purple-red blotches; there were burst blood vessels and ridges that oozed pus, a few open sores on his buttocks and shoulder blades.

Het ziet er niet so best uit, I said, maar maakt u zich geen zorgen, wij komen er wel uit.

*

And what does Kasper do next in this fairy tale, colleagues? He purchases salves and oils and balms at the pharmacy. He goes to the Hema and buys new white clothes, a new coat and shoes and the most nutritious ingredients for an invalid's meals. And here I must mention a remarkable writerly invention: Kasper describes pushing his two tables together, the one of musings and the other of science, the poetry table and the prose table, covering them in white towels, setting up his reading lamp like the light in an operating theatre. He helped the naked swan whisperer onto the tables, and set about tending to him from head to toe, three times a day, fourteen days in a row.

I could not read any further.

This, then, was the third time I put away the letter. This time I stashed it with my teaching materials, along with the white dummy book, because I thought I might use it to explain the problems of magical realism to my junior students. Not that I ever did; I was busy with other things. My novel had been translated, the translation checked and approved. There was a short respite in my own writing obligations and I decided to give my house a spring-clean, to have the place painted and pruned, have the squirrels removed from the attic, set a trap for the mouse, and let my wrist heal.

But then, about a month later, the clean-up in full swing, the letter all but forgotten – the mimic book unread, the cassettes unplayed – I received a third shipment, an oddly thick envelope in my postbox.

I tore open the envelope, standing there surrounded by painters from Wonder Wall in their white overalls. It was filled with sand – a good handful of pure white sand fell onto my feet. I remember stepping back and staring for quite some time at my two dark footprints on the paving. I sent the workmen home for the day. Who could have sent me an envelope full of sand, who but Kasper Olwagen? I checked the back of the envelope: no sender, just a scribble made with something like a stick of charcoal, the name Dwarsrivier.

Why Dwarsrivier – "cross river"? Some allegorical joke? Maybe his letter, which I still had not finished reading after all that time, would hold some clue? Maybe I should have a closer look at the logbook? And then there were also the tapes I had not listened to, in the Woolworths bag in my broom cupboard. I gathered all Kasper's missives together on the kitchen table.

First, I picked up the letter and read on from page twenty, where I stopped the last time. Let me summarise the story for you.

After a month's worth of skin treatments, the drifter's hide had healed, his hair was cut, his scent pleasantly human. But this was not enough. Kasper was obsessed with getting the swan whisperer to talk. Because he was jealous of him, jealous of his art of communication with the "birds of the underworld", as he put it. At night, he watched over the dozing vagabond, logbook in hand in case the man talked in his sleep, but all he heard was the ticking of the radiator, the rain pattering against the windows, the bell of Sint Nicolaas striking. Kasper could not handle the man's silence. If he could just get him to open his mouth, even if just to say at dinner, and I quote: "Please pass the salt", he would be able to start questioning him about how he charmed the swans.

Pass the salt, ladies and gentlemen? I had to smile. The story did not operate at this level of realism. I was starting to feel that my student was building an argument, that he was making some sort of case. Because the things he did to try to get the man to speak sounded like a programme, a via dolorosa with stations of the cross, and this letter was addressed to me, to the student whisperer, if you will.

But I never replied.

This is the first time I have ever spoken about it.

Let me stick to the story. How did Mr Philanthropist try to get his wayward guest talking? First, he sat him down in front of the television for hours on end, trying to provoke him with images of broken knees in Kenya, the terror of the long knives in Zimbabwe, the mourning polar bears of the North Pole, the smouldering trees of the Amazon; when this did not work, he made him climb through the roof hatch on clear evenings and showed him the swan and the harp in the stars, the tears of Orpheus in the west; and when this had no effect, he made him listen to every romantic swansong he could lay his hands on in the library – Grieg, Sibelius, Tchaikovsky. All for nothing. Not the terrors of our own time, not the eternal signature of the firmament, not the dated melodies of the Romantic era nor a glass of wine from Burgundy, nothing could untie this tramp's tongue. Kasper writes that he considered taking him to a psychiatrist, or an ear, nose and throat specialist. One morning he examined the swan whisperer's mouth himself, only to find there a healthy, light-red tongue, the clapper firmly strapped to the root, as he writes. He continues:

I shone the light into the back of his throat. The tonsils hung on either side of the uvula like two smaller bells. I ran the tip of my index finger along the roof of his mouth. Its ridges reminded me of a harp.

But the harps would not sound, at least not in Kasper's writing. What he wrote were rows and columns, records and registrations, in shorthand throughout; an almost pathological writer's block, this much at least was clear to me from the logbook. The entry for January 5th, 2003, was the following, in full sentences, the only semblance of self-reflection.

Conider ↓

Swannyboy is standing like a statue behind my chair while I am trying to write, been like that for hours, as if he is supervising me, I pretend not to know he is there but I am listening, what is it that I hear? Just the sounds of the city? The sibilance of his blood? Or my own? He does not know that I can see his reflection in the glass of the picture on the wall, I can see his lips moving, and I move my pen over the page as well as I can, in sync with what I imagine him to be saying. What does my pen remind me of? The graphite needle in a weather station, registering all moisture and wind and cloud movement and recording them on a roll of graph paper.

And this, colleagues, is followed by rows and rows of sounds, the phonological patterns of Afrikaans. Some examples show the influence of the Khoi languages. Spak, grak, spal, malk, olk, skolk, and then mrie !krie krakadouw. Some of them were randomly strung together and arranged into what I can only call sound limericks. Transcriptions of what Kasper seemingly thought the swan whisperer was saying, or dreamt or invented. Swan whisperings, in other words. And what does the language of swans sound like?

> *Rie mrie, rapuu,*
> *kriep, !tewiek, miruu,*
> *tohoe wa bohoe*
> *askla mor usa,*
> *pierok griemok sklahoe.*

Although I am a fan of nonsense verse, often finding in it more pleasure than in the pompous loftiness of, say, "Groot Ode" by Van Wyk Louw, I was in no mood to be made a fool of by a psychotic student looking for a mother. I smacked the book shut.

Look, Professor, a deaf and dumb schizophrenic taught me more about the art of writing than you could! And then pages filled with mocking rhymes. I should have known it was not innocent. A year or so later, I found the phrase "tohoe wa bohoe" in a book about the Pentateuch. It is Hebrew for the formless void in Genesis.

This I leave with you for now. I still do not know what to make of it. But something just occurred to me which I – well, someone in my line of work – would rather forget, but which might bring clarity.

It relates to an incident from the time when Kasper was still a registered student, the only time he dared contradict me. I had summoned him for feedback on his latest piece of writing. I wished to conclude it briskly. He had barely taken his seat when I fired away. Drop the metaphysics, Kasper, I said, drop the ideas, write what the readers want, a juicy story about your hometown, a tale of unwelcome newcomers, gang violence, dog fights, highway robbery, shebeens, self-importance, adultery, braaivleis, family feuds, Maggie Laubser and piety. Call it *The Sorrow of Rustling River.*

Kasper's eyes glazed over; his voice was thin when he spoke:

And a smug local author as narrator? The days of cosy local realism are over, in case you had not noticed, he said, even when it is dressed up in all sorts of metafictional drag. If I were to write prose one day, it would be plain street reports, pavement anthropology, recorded from a perspective of distant sympathy. Clean and dry.

I saw small bubbles of spittle at the corners of his mouth. His hand was inside his blazer, but he did not take out his pen.

Fiction, he continued, with his tongue dragging more than usual, fiction can no longer console us. The terrors of our fatherland rob the narrative imagination of its will, its willpower. We can no longer imagine anything. We must become brutalists, collectors of facts, no longer storytellers, but archivists of the unimaginable brutalities of our country. From this, readers will gather for themselves fear and empathy, perhaps even entertainment and knowledge.

Well, this was the first time I had ever felt I was learning something from a student. I did not question him further about his views; I was not about to admit I was impressed. To be honest, I was jealous of what I recognised as an angle for a new literary movement in Afrikaans literature, which had become so woefully stuck in adventure and self-portrayal.

Mr Olwagen, I said, I regret to say that I think you feign bravery. When I look at you, I see no brutalist, I see an aesthete. I do not see lists of necklace murders, raped children, murdered geriatrics, armed robberies. What I do see are lists of fauna and flora, Lehmann lovegrass, heart-seed lovegrass, stagger grass, fountain grass, quaking grass. Should you not stay true to your nature? You read Adorno's aesthetics theories; I fail to see in you a taste for critical analysis, or for satirical commentary on your fatherland. I look at your twitching nostrils and your hand on your heart and I see someone who feels overwhelmed, weak, scared, alone, not someone willing to give himself a death sentence in sixteen lines, like your much admired Osip Mandelstam did with his poem about everybody's beloved Onkel Stalin. Or like Breytenbach did in his poem for the butcher. Like no poet today would dare to write about Robert Mugabe. You have a lazy tongue, Olwagen. You are a symptom of the problem that besets progressive intellectuals in this country. Politically correct pose on the one hand and evasive behaviour on the other. Get a life, I would say.

He kept staring at me with that inflamed gaze of his, but I did not return the look; I have no time for this kind of behaviour in students.

Be honest, I said, how can you be a pavement anthropologist on any interesting pavement in this country today without an armed bodyguard by your side?

And when I got no reaction: Your kind has been outlawed in this country, I said; there is always someone who needs a bow tie when a pig is being butchered.

I stood up behind my desk. He had to get this clearly. I would leave no room for misunderstanding.

Mister Olwagen, I said, do you want to know what I see when I look at you? I see someone who wants to banish himself to the sticks, yes, to the back of beyond, to become an architect of the intensified moment in the unblemished outdoors, a sculptor in the amber of words. You want to become an animal in your language, the way a genet is himself in the undergrowth. All very nice, mind you. I see your dictum, it is written all over your imposing forehead: The only subversive deed remaining in a superficial, brutalised society is the cultivation of the intimate discomfort of the lyric. True or false? Or would you formulate your escapist desires differently?

I could see that he was having difficulty. But honestly, what teacher has never upset a student? Not that you mean to, but you cannot do much about it when a student feels crushed. Nonetheless, this is not how an educator should act. Later, I sought advice from a colleague about the matter and he reminded me that Kasper was a client of a corporate institution, and that going forward I should treat him as such, no more and no less. I was his knowledge partner. If he wished not to complete his course, I should leave him be, that is all, it is his own choice, as long as he pays for services rendered.

*

Where was I? I have lost my thread. Oh yes, I was at the nonsense, the nonsense poems Olwagen had written in the mock-up. Tohoe wa bohoe. The formless void.

We were discussing the third package, the sand in the envelope. Dwarsrivier. I got out my atlas and, lo and behold, there it was, no allegories here, a real Dwarsrivier in the Cederberg Mountains, a farm belonging to the Nieuwoudt clan, closest post office Clanwilliam. I took the dustpan and brush, swept up the sand on the garden path and poured it back into the envelope. For the purposes of this lecture I have put it into this hourglass.

You understand the situation. Kasper's letter from the hospital was nothing less than an instruction manual. I had to return to this letter every time in order to make sense of the ensuing packages. Was I trapped in the revenge plan of a wronged man? Or had I been caught by a tall tale? You see, I still did not believe the whole story of the swan whisperer.

You look at me? You ask, at what point might one start to think that such a tale could be true after all? That Kasper had not made any of it up? That the whole swan-whispering business actually happened that way, exactly, word for word?

There I sat at my kitchen table, drinking cup after cup of coffee, going through Kasper's densely written pages. There was a teeth-pulling scene on page fifty. Perhaps the man has dental difficulties, Kasper writes, maybe that is why he would not talk. So he took his lodger to the dentist, where three teeth were pulled that same day, and numerous fillings administered. And then follows the part of the letter that got me thinking that perhaps my student had actually experienced something preposterous. Unlikely events occur far more readily, as we all know, in the real world than they do in stories.

On the night of 20 January, after the teeth had been pulled, I woke with a draught on my neck. The swan whisperer was at the open window in his pyjamas, arms raised. I slipped down the stairs behind his back. Outside on the canal in front of my apartment there were, believe it or not, not one or two but dozens of swans, the entire length of the Geldersekade, nodding and swishing – necks bowing, stretching, curving, a kind of writing in which the white cursive danced on the black ink of the canal. They came swimming from beneath the bridge, from the Oosterdok they swarmed, the air alive with the whirring of their wings. With their long necks set back they landed among one another, flapping and splashing. I was dumbfounded at the steadily growing congregation of stalklike necks, the feathers royally displayed in a massed nocturnal plume, the surface of the water astir under the blue light from the Liebherr cranes. This is how it must have looked when the gods herded all the swans together to pull the sled of Orpheus.

Professor, he asks me here in brackets, *what would you call a drift of swans in Afrikaans? A "drifsel"? Could one call them a swathe? A throng? A longing, a sin, a shame of swans?*

I did not return to the flat that evening, he writes. *I wandered around the city, too perturbed by the spectacle of swans, all my doubts, all my reservations about this drifter summarily eliminated. He was a genius. Autistic, perhaps, as in* Rain Man, *but still a genius. Did you see it? The movie with Dustin Hoffman in the lead? I had to find a different approach. But how? He could not exactly take me on as his apprentice. Nor as the scribe of his whisperings. And no, I understood that I was not his saviour, nor his interpreter. Nor his lover, although that would have been a sweet ending for my story.*

By six the next morning, tired and cold and hungry, I finally knew what to do. Why had it taken me so long? I had to go back to the flat and switch on the kettle. At a quarter to seven I had to knock on his door, open the curtains and touch his shoulder to wake him, just as I had done every morning for the past two and a half months. I would have to sit on the chair by his bed and have coffee with him in the sleepy silence, while we listened to the city slowly waking, the train wheels scouring the tracks, the siren in the Oosterdok announcing another workday. Together we had to sit there while the morning glow filled the room and a lone sparrow started chirping in the gutter on the roof, waiting for the bells to strike seven, first the Oude Kerk on De Wallen and then, after two strokes, the Zuiderkerk, and then promptly the closer clangour of Sint Nicolaas, as its dorsal fins were slowly sketched in before our eyes by the morning light. And then I would touch my face to see if I had to shave, and from the corner of my eye I would see him doing the same, with a barely audible scratching sound. And all of this, I knew, I would be able to do that morning for the first time without anxiety, because I understood that, after everything, and despite his unusual abilities, I had simply become his friend, the friend of this singular man, Professor, was that too much to ask?

Well, dear listeners, I cannot expect you to fully understand, after sharing with you only a few extracts from this letter, how moved I was by this passage. Sitting at my kitchen table, I knew without a doubt that all of it was true.

True and poignant. Because when Kasper got back to the flat that morning with his newfound insight, it was too late: His friend was gone, missing, rope ladder and all. And yet there was more. Page sixty-three.

He was disconsolate, Kasper writes, utterly inconsolable and distressed. Just when he had finally realised what was important about the swan whisperer – not his Orphean arts, but his ordinary bodily presence as a housemate – he disappeared. Gone, missing. For days on end, Kasper looked for him, up and down the swan route. He searched every night shelter, enquired at every welfare society. Asked every *Daklozenkrant* seller: "Heeft u een man gezien met wit haar en een touwladder?" He distributed flyers across the whole city: "Vriend vermist".

And so, in the course of searching for his friend, Kasper himself becomes a drifter. Day and night, in wind and rain, he walks the city in the threadbare coat, wearing the boots of the swan whisperer. And here we find beautiful descriptions of Amsterdam, the reflections, the gables, the elms, the trams, always with the notion: I am no longer seeking inspiration or authorial fulfilment, I am looking for my friend, and every street corner and every reflection and every bridge speaks of my longing. Kasper writes – and this is where the angels start dancing, where in my view Kasper becomes a writer – of how he lingered at every bridge where he used to find the swan whisperer, raising his hands in the air and murmuring: What did I do wrong to lose my mate? And that if the swans did appear then, it would be immaterial.

Let me read you the final page.

I believe I spotted him once, white hair ahead of me on the bustling pavement, and I was gripped by the conviction that I should not call out or run after him, that if he were to look around and see me, I would be lost. I sensed that I myself had been followed for some time, in fact by someone who thought that they, too, recognised me. I realised I was part of a procession through the city, a silent convoy of the urban lost and looking, all of us connected at the wrist by an endless black ribbon, all of us thinking that perhaps we have found a lost person, someone who had run away, but afraid to make this hope known, afraid of being disappointed, rather walking on in the solace of a community of like-minded individuals, the consolation of not being alone, of belonging to the most unbreakable brotherhood on earth: the ones who stayed on, who have survived, who have been left behind.

And so, dear listeners, Kasper ends at the beginning, in the portico across from his own home where he saw his whisperer for the very first time. He falls asleep there, hungry and exhausted, at a degree or two below freezing. He slips into a coma. The city police pick him up and deliver him to the hospital, as he puts it: *Without name, without papers, with only my story and the need to tell it to the one person on earth who would understand.*

After two months and no further unusual parcels, I bought a new cassette player, packed up Kasper's tapes and travelled to the Cederberg. The deeper I went into the mountains, from the Gydo Pass all the way through towards Clanwilliam, the more I felt I was on the right track. I found the farm Dwarsrivier easily and unpacked at a campground called Sanddrif. The sand in Kasper's envelope was exactly the same as the sand I found at the river there. At night I listened to the tapes in my tent, fifty-three distinguishable recitations. I came to the conclusion that they were poems, recorded close to running water, or in the mouth of waving grass, as though Kasper wanted to provide his voice with a kind of pedal point, not the bold bass pedal he heard in the work of Bach, but rustling, murmuring, as though time was an instrument played by the transparent fingers of grass and water. I walked up and down the river for days, carrying my cassette player, until I found what I was looking for, a specific minor murmuring of water over flat rock at a small whirlpool, and also a patch of reeds with white plumes that rustled silkily like Chinese cymbals. These were the background sounds that Kasper had chosen to mask his voice.

Pale, oversensitive Kasper, how cold he must have been in those bare gorges in winter, beside that dark stream! There where he bowed to the wind, to the water, with his song. Would he have hung his bow tie on a reed? His waistcoat on an aloe, emptied his fountain pen onto the sand?

However hard I listened – and, ladies and gentlemen, I am still listening, I will never stop listening – I could not make out the words of the poems. If they were even words. What I could hear clearly was the strong commencement of the theme, and then its countermovement, varied somewhat in vowels and consonants, reinforced and built up by repetition and refrain, magnificent edifices of sound. I could catch rhythms, rhythmic variations, the length and cadence of the lines, their inversions and elongations and enrichments, the climaxes, the accelerations and decelerations. Also the tone and feeling of each recitation, sometimes elegiac and legato, sometimes exuberant, often painfully ecstatic, always with a songlike quality. I could understand the argument of the sounds, or rather the research done via sound, the search for possible developments or variations of the central theme, but never the meaning.

My work, I know, is measured out for the rest of my life. I am the real dummy, you see, the mock-up professor, and god only knows who is writing in me. Someone has fitted me with a tongue. My just deserts, I would say, if that person is my missing student or his missing friend. But I will not give up; it is bad enough that two people have vanished without trace. I sit in my yard and the seasons pass above me. I no longer write novels; I have come to see myself as a translator. I study the lists of compound sounds that Kasper recorded in my book, my empty parting gift to him. Using them, I make one translation after another of his sound poems. As soon as I finish one, I read it in unison with the sound patterns in the corresponding recording, and I keep working on it until it matches his voice as closely as possible. Much is lost in this process; perhaps something is gained. I drop the adjectives, I scrap the ideas, I barely link words to meaning, because meaning is irrelevant. What is important is the materiality of the words. They must become like grains of sand, inconsequential in weight; sweet, white, dry sand that does not care if you let it slip through your fingers. Twice a year I go to the Cederberg Mountains, to that whirlpool, that patch of marsh reeds, and I read my latest translations aloud there, in the hope that the water and the rushes will keep whispering it, perhaps whisper it through to him, if he is still somewhere out there.

Shall I share my latest attempt with you? I dedicate it to my lost student, the one who taught me everything a writer should *be* – which is, mind you, something quite different to what a writer should *write*.

Morning of the Southern Boubou

Holy crack! slipped from the knuckles
of this side's foodfiddler and domesticator,
the shrike flits through daybreak's crevice,
ama-a-a-a-zed at the spice of his cinnamon chest,
under his clove claws the rock 'n' roll rippin'
spick 'n spark spillin' crossriversands,
tincture of peck flecked on his coat-tails and flanks,
fixed in his frock, top hat trimmed
he frolicks over acres to the water's edge, look!
triiiiiiiiilllllions of big and small shrikes in the looking glass,
cut it out, you cohorts of chancers in the ripples
that he counters with a cocky akimbo,
quicktailin' the kidlight in the riverine herb,
and sidesteps, see here, this swi-sh-sh-shy oldcart waistcoat,
he is the one and only goddodger
here in the tendertipped noonteasing sun
!toweak in his throttle sits his petname !toweak
like a bell in the mount cunt, a-rou-ou-ou-sed
by the mouthsoft morn.[ii]

43

The Percussionist

A Eulogy

I was dead, then alive.
Weeping, then laughing.

The power of love came into me,
and I became fierce like a lion,
then tender like the evening star.

He said, "You're not mad enough.
You don't belong in this house."

I went wild and had to be tied up.
He said, "Still not wild enough
to stay with us!"

I broke through another layer
into joyfulness.

He said, "It's not enough."
I died.

He said, "You're a clever little man,
full of fantasy and doubting."

I plucked out my feathers and became a fool.
He said, "Now you're the candle
for this assembly."

But I'm no candle. Look!
I'm scattered smoke.

He said, "You are the sheikh, the guide."
But I'm not a teacher. I have no power.

He said, "You already have wings.
I cannot give you wings."

But I wanted *his* wings.
I felt like some flightless chicken.

Then new events said to me,
"Don't move. A sublime generosity is
coming toward you."

And old love said, "Stay with me."

I said, "I will."

You are the fountain of the sun's light.
I am a willow shadow on the ground.
You make my raggedness silky.

The soul at dawn is like darkened water
that slowly begins to say *Thank you, thank you.*

Then at sunset, again, Venus gradually
changes into the moon and then the whole nightsky.

This comes of smiling back
at your smile.

The chess master says nothing,
other than moving the silent chess piece.

That I am part of the ploys
of this game makes me
amazingly happy.

*

Honourable friends – the left-behind, like myself; Mevrouw
Oldemarkt. For thirty years I knew your brother Willem. The text
I just quoted was always pinned up on the wall in his kitchen. It's
from the work of the thirteenth-century Sufi mystic Rumi and it's
about . . . well, what is it about? About smoke, about wings, about
shadows? I've never understood it, but since Willem's passing last
week I've read it again and again. It's like an old garment that's
become soft and trustworthy with much wear, like this coat I'm
wearing before you today, and this hat, and this old brown shirt.
They all belonged to Willem. Tweedledee and Tweedledum, the
two of us, that's what Willem always said. One goes to sleep
while the other stays up.

I don't wear a watch myself, Mevrouw, you must help me, please – it's my understanding that the auditorium has been booked for the afternoon, and I have a good forty-five minutes to speak? But I notice that the chapel's clock has stopped on twelve o'clock . . . a prop, perhaps? Well, that's what I feel like here under the dimmed lights, in front of these curtains, on the black marble: a prop, Jacob Kippelstein of Kippelstein en Zoon, antiquarian on the Spiegelgracht, specialising in grandfather clocks. Speeches are not my strong suit. Ohne Schatten ist draußen die Welt.

I am here, as Mevrouw Oldemarkt can confirm, because the author asked in his last will and testament that I should give an overview of his work at his funeral. He wanted to be remembered for his books, he always said, because nobody would be able to make any sense of his life. Not that I understand everything he wrote – I'm a technician, not a literary scholar. To me, the inscriptions matter most. "To my dearly beloved craftsman Kippelstein, the tick-tock man. Trustingly, your friend Willem Oldemarkt", he wrote in the front of the first copy of every new book before giving it to me.

But perhaps I wasn't the first, or the only one. All of us gathered here in the chapel this afternoon know that Willem was a loner who carefully kept his acquaintances in the dark about each other. There may be others here who first got to know him, as I did, as a face behind a pair of binoculars. Here around my neck is the Zeiss with which he spied on somebody during our last afternoon together, a week ago today. I wish to tell you about that afternoon.

Here in my hand I have the story he was working on at the time. The title: "The Percussionist", and in brackets: "Black Pages", full of additions and deletions. Black as the first matter, that's how Willem described his work in progress.

He stipulated that none of his unfinished work may be published. But how can I keep this story to myself? Verdreh' dir doch den eig'nen Kopf, Mann, you may be thinking, but to whom else can I turn? With your permission, then, Mevrouw, the clock is ticking, let me begin.

*

A week ago, Wednesday afternoon, 13 August, was the last time I saw Willem. I was in a bad mood, bristling with the kind of insights one gains when travelling alone in foreign lands for any length of time. I'd just returned from two and a half months abroad, having undertaken an archaeological tour of the antique water clocks of the Old World. My work was behind schedule, and I'd had to interrupt urgent repairs to a Louis XIV mantel clock to schlepp across the city to the Jordaan, to Willem's new place, which he'd moved into while I was away. He'd already called me the night before, oblivious to the normal working hours I keep to maintain the precarious balance between work and life.

Please come, Jacob, he said, I can't finish this new story on my own, I feel weak.

I was barely through the door when he launched right into it.

He didn't even ask about my trip. When the percussionist completed his masterpiece the evening before, he said, they'd both wept bitterly. But his tears, Willem's, were of "inferior quality" because he shed them into his binoculars, gazing across the courtyard so as not to miss any of the young man's "ecstasy and despair".

Slow down, slow down, I said, I'm not following, what are you on about?

All I have in life, Willem said, as he hung my coat on his crowded coatrack, are the small victories of my characters in the midst of the oceans of misery that engulf them.

All you have in life is spying on other lives, I muttered to the floorboards. I had to untie my shoelaces because my feet were swollen from walking all the way from the Spiegelgracht to Westerstraat, a problem I'd picked up on my trip, standing around in museums.

Before we could settle down at his messy writing table, Willem's foot caught on the carpet and he grabbed my arm to keep from falling.

Kippelstein, he said, I'm feeling light-headed.

Light-headed? I asked. Surely an essential requirement for a writer?

He pretended not to hear me. I led him to his chair and sat down facing him. His gaze was bewildered, a muscle in his cheek twitching. I thought he was going to say that he'd missed me, but instead he said: This story about the percussionist is a self-portrait, Jacob, how can I do it justice?

justие

You can do any <u>Scheißerei</u>, but whether it's just, you'll have to judge for yourself, I said, to which he simply raised his eyebrows.

This was the first time I'd heard about the percussionist. Not that this was remarkable in itself. His novels teemed with characters with unusual occupations. The <u>fortune-teller</u>, the <u>bee-keeper</u>, the <u>porcelain tiler</u>, and now the <u>percussionist</u>. No doubt another young man, I thought, who didn't come close to deserving his attention.

I'm not much of a fan of percussion myself, I said. Give me a stirring melody any day.

Don't be so pitiless, watchmaker, Willem said. This story about the percussionist, if I can get it right, the way I've dreamt it, it will pulverise into splinters the armoire of ordinary human language.

How many times had I heard this? But secretly, I was relieved. Once he got going with his "pulverising", he left me in peace and I could continue with my clocks undisturbed.

But that afternoon, we were still in the initial phase of the new story, the "dark night of the soul", as Willem called it, and on top of that, he kept filling my glass with bad wine. Every time he came with yet another demonstration of his percussionist story, I took a gulp to hide my irritation. Did he really not care about the <u>clepsydra</u> in the Tower of the Winds at Kyros, or the representation of the water clock of Al-Jazari in the Topkapi Palace Museum in Istanbul? But already he was far gone, in his own world, playing out something that he himself didn't yet understand. He began by tapping a pencil against his front teeth, remarking that here, God help us, is the one place you can see the skeleton poking through the flesh.

I took off my shoes and settled into the chair I always sat in to hear him out, an ocean of densely inscribed and struck-through pages between us on the table, with brass pestles and mortars as paperweights. He picked up the manuscript and gripped the edge of the table with his other hand for the introduction: In the first week in my new residence, he read, I was extremely upset because every afternoon at exactly twenty-five minutes past five a most tremendous thundering of drums would break loose.

He looked at me like a conqueror about to enter virgin territory.

Na und, alter Hund, I thought, and on *this* you would base the kingdom of heavenly harmony? But I knew when to keep quiet.

My eyes skimmed over the chaos in Willem's house, with its usual lack of clear demarcation between areas for sleeping, eating and writing. Dirty glasses everywhere, books, papers, immeasurable quantities of bric-a-brac. It was even worse than usual, because I'd been away when he moved in and couldn't help him unpack and organise his things. To get my attention, he rapped the edge of the table with a ruler. The drumming, he continued, had clearly been discussed with all the other tenants in the block, everyone except him, the newcomer; as far as he could see, using his binoculars to peer into the living rooms and kitchens that faced onto the courtyard, everyone else went on with their normal nightly activities despite the Gewalt. Nobody as much as looked up, he said. Not Mrs Steen van den Heuvel, kneading a meatball mixture on her countertop at her own long-suffering pace, not Mr Broeksma, pouring himself a jenever on the folding lid of his drinks cabinet, still less the twins Hinderix and Winderix as they spun their yo-yos up and down over the balustrade; no, not even the heron that slept in the beech tree at night paid any heed to the racket.

Didn't your earplugs help? I asked, knowing very well that he suffered from tinnitus, which made him sensitive to something as small as a dripping tap or a loose roofing sheet in the wind.

He got up, opened the window and motioned me closer. He put his hand on my neck and bent me over the windowsill. Holding my head there, he covered my eyes with the other hand until he was satisfied that I'd appreciated the silence of his court-yard. Listen, he said, the far-off buzz of the city, like the sea in a shell. And then he shook a box of matches in front of my nose so that I could hear it echoing around the courtyard. Wonderful, do you hear? Like a cough in a cathedral.

And indeed, in that fair courtyard with the statuesque beech at its centre, regular drum solos would drive any normal city dweller, even one without sensitive ears, to apoplexy.

Again, he filled our glasses. What I shouldn't ask, I knew, was: How old is he, your drummer? And I'd better not call him a "drummer", either, since in Willem's mind he was already cloaked in the radiance of the timpanist in a symphony orchestra.

It was the same old story. I couldn't help but think of the paver of four years before. How long did Willem gaze at him, research the sound of trowels, read everything about paving? How long before the paver got wind of it and got annoyed? Two, three months? And then the struggle to complete the story about the whole thing, and at length the next house move, with me helping him, once again, to pack up lock, stock and barrel. This had become a fixed pattern in Willem's life, and in my life with Willem, if I may put it like that, Mevrouw. Each time I had to help him bury another lost love.

I rubbed the spot where he'd gripped my neck. I felt like telling him what I thought about all of this, once and for all. But he saw it coming, and spoke before I could start: Don't spoil my story before hearing me out, please, this one is about . . .

I understand, I said with a straight face, it's about a corpse, it's another eulogy. You seem concerned, Mevrouw? No need, I'm not here to dishonour your brother's memory, rather to admit to my own shortcomings. I ask for your patience. I must relate the backstory, otherwise you won't understand the events that unfolded that afternoon.

For a whole week, Willem told me, he'd studied the windows on the other side with his binoculars – yes, dear listeners, with this very Zeiss around my neck, made for big-game hunters, a high-fidelity instrument with minimal distortion and crystal lenses – until he finally came to the conclusion that the percussionist must be obscured by the beech tree. So he disguised himself as a "municipal tree surgeon", and at the appropriate hour gained access to the courtyard through a house on the ground floor, in order to locate the "hold of the young god". He sawed a peephole in the tree, he told me, so as to observe the "percussive ouvrage" through a "keyhole of foliage". Every evening, he'd take his position at his window on the courtyard and watch the young man through the leaves: "slender, tawny blond, with finely chiselled features, something shiny in his left ear".

Let me read from the manuscript. Could one of your staff help me with the light here on the lectern? Oh, here's the switch, thank you, Mevrouw, you're very kind. Here is a fragment about the art of the drummer:

With his right foot he set the basic rhythm on the bass-drum pedal, a rapid disco beat, boom-boom-boom-boom, and then reined it in with the sibilant little splash-cymbal, before introducing more rhythms on the floor drum and the rototoms, and once that got going, when he'd come up to the right tempo, he'd finally start slamming the crash cymbal, the ride cymbal and the hi-hat for emphasis until his ears were ringing and he had to put on a pair of red mufflers, playing faster and faster still for the rest of his rehearsal, until his foot slipped from the pedal and the whole rhythmic edifice collapsed, after which he'd usually take off his shirt and light a cigarette, and finish the session sweating and smoking in a cadenza that would end at precisely six o'clock with careening cymbals, a turbulent bass, and drumrolls in all directions, until the drumsticks shot apart in a shower of splinters.

Through the open window, the racket in the courtyard sounded, as Willem describes it here, like the "approach through a barley field of cohorts of harnessed knights on the heels of the horseman with the clacking jawbone".

Schon gut, I said, not moving a muscle.

I felt his gaze upon me as he tried to work out what I was really thinking.

You're staring at me like someone divining coffee dregs, I said. Do go on.

He glared at me, remarked that one probably couldn't expect a more interesting response from a watchmaker. I should rather keep quiet, he said, until I'd heard the end of the story, before commenting again on his gaze. Who did I think I was, he asked, to diminish with these barbs a story shared in greatest confidence by a lifelong friend? Then he yanked the ash pan from the fireplace and hit it with the poker, one almighty bang, like the moon gong in a Zen monastery. Like this, boom!

A eulogist who slams his palm on the lectern? Did I frighten you? A lifeless funeral, Willem always said, would be like writing a boring book about boredom. No damage to the lectern, see. You're smiling, Mevrouw? I can see that you share your brother's sense of humour.

In the silence after the poker bang, I composed myself by doing a tour of Willem's new place, the twentieth or so that he'd called home. He hadn't finished unpacking, it seemed; but I should've suspected, already at that early point in the afternoon, that every object in the apparent mess had been positioned with a very specific purpose in mind. You see, Willem always described himself as a realist. In his work, he paid intense attention to the representation of space; every detail had to fulfil a specific function in the "total design", and as far as possible he'd try out every spatial mechanism himself before finalising it in the text. Shoemakers go barefoot, my father always said; similarly, there was no sign of total design in Willem's daily life.

You're nodding, Mevrouw? You're familiar with this scenario? Pots and pans full of musty water on the stove, empty wine bottles by the bin, rolls of unopened magazines and newspapers on the floor. There was a collection of olive-oil tins on a cupboard in the corner of the kitchen, from all the places he'd travelled to in his younger days. Every time he moved, they went along, as though to remind him that he was still the same person. They were stacked in three pyramids that day, but I didn't ask why, because I saw from the corner of my eye that he was scribbling busily in the margins of his manuscript: "rehearsal notes", as he called them.

Rehearsal, a favourite word of Willem's, the practice session directly preceding a premiere. With my "unwavering tact", I was, according to him, his "official rehearser", a title that referred not only to my discretion as a listener, but also to my "tick-tock talent". You see, I repair metronomes in my spare time and therefore I had to help him prepare, but for what?

Watch the tempo, Herr Poltergeist, tick-tock, tick-tock, keep the beat, bind the measure, I will see to the greater design, he'd call out when he let his freewheeling sentences loose on me. He said that he couldn't do anything without me as "pacesetter". I was an inspiration for someone in his line of work, he said, such was the apparent perfectionism of the professional horologist, my insistence on functionality, my supposed sense for the synchronisation of all parts, paired with my unfailing aesthetic of clock face and pendulum. He was excellent at flattery when he wanted something from me. Flattery and jest. Love with feeling, that's what he called it.

But honestly, I felt more guinea pig than inspiration that afternoon. I had to duck as I navigated past six mobiles hanging from the ceiling in his living room. He called them "The Oldemarkt Galaxies", "candelabras of inconsolability", and he was always working on them, adding or replacing elements. Marbles, crystals, parrot bells, pods, crackers, wind-blown seeds, teaspoons. And sheaves of old compact discs that cast specks of light all over his "Ali Baba's cave". More spares for his mobiles were stored in wooden boxes and tea tins with neat labels indicating their contents: keys, bottle caps, nails.

Willem, as you will know, Mevrouw, collected everything he saw; his pockets were always too small, his suitcase too heavy. He called this collection his "encyclopaedia of non-recurring objects".

Everything you touch, Kippelstein, you turn into clockwork, he often said to me, and everything I gather, I hang in my "baldaquin of lost moments". Chronos and Kairos we are, the two faces of time.

Oh, come off it, I always said, more like Boruch and Zoruch, Knödel und Suppe.

I felt more and more uncomfortable that afternoon in Willem's new home on Westerstraat. He sat there watching me intently as I stood fiddling with the contents of one of his tea tins, buttons of all sizes and colours. Did I want to hear the rest of the story, he asked, making another note in his Black Book. It would be an honour, I said, to hear what happened next with the little drum major across the courtyard of unfulfilled longing. I put the tin back in its spot on the shelf and returned to my chair by the window. Willem seemed sad, even desperate. There was no other way; I just had to let it wash over me.

*

Every morning at seven, Willem told me, the percussionist left his apartment with a bag containing a pair of blue overalls, safety boots, a hard hat and a lunchbox. And he arrived home every afternoon at quarter past five, drank a beer, ate a packet of pretzels and then sat down behind the drum kit at twenty-five past five to start practising. Except for the improvisations at the end of each session, there was nothing in the young man's playing that indicated "rhythmic ambition", as far as he could see. And so, he wasn't surprised when one evening by half past five, no sound had come from across the courtyard. It was dead quiet, just the drone of the city in the enclosure.

Willem went quiet, brought to his eyes the binoculars that lay on the table between us, aimed them across the courtyard, put them back down and looked at me.

Not a sound, Jacob, complete silence at half past five, he repeated, looking at me quizzically. This was my cue: I had to guess why it was silent.

They'd brought him back on a stretcher, he'd fallen from a Liebherr crane, I ventured, le petit ange bien tombé . . .

Willem shook his head.

No? I said, then it must be a builders' holiday.

Kippelstein, you're the most prosaic poltergeist I've ever seen, Willem said.

Fine, I said, let me not roll away the stone and unseal the tomb. Three Days of Silence. And then? A blond resurrection?

Willem wiped his forehead. He drew the manuscript closer, with some difficulty. His hands were trembling. The wrists, I noticed for the first time, were thin in his old brown flannel shirt, the one he always wore when starting a new story. You're nodding, Mevrouw? You know that old shirt? Its sleeves are too long for me.

Three days of silence, Willem continued, and then, late on the afternoon of the fourth day, at five forty-five, an "Orphean sibilation of cymbals" rang out in the courtyard. He adjusted his binoculars and peered into the percussionist's room through the "bronze foliage of the bobbing beech". A naked young Asian girl was sitting behind the drums, "brown as molasses" with long black hair. She was stroking the drums with a red poppy. And on the bed, also naked, resting against the headboard, drawing on a cigarette, the percussionist. Utterly sated from the "excesses of carnal love", as far as could be seen.

Och, Willem, I said, is this really necessary?

Don't "och" me, he said. Of course I could put it differently, but it's for your sake, because you have no view of these kinds of extravagances in real life, except when they're framed by the windows of fiction I open for you.

It's not easy, being a writer's friend. Through the windows of fiction, a view of the hidden dimensions of life? What hypocrisy! In just the same way, he'd looked at *me* through his binoculars thirty years ago, and had known exactly what I was doing at my table in the studio on the top floor of our shop on the Spiegelgracht.

But this wasn't the right moment to remind him of that. I studied the label on the empty wine bottle, and said that I'd had Côtes du Rhône that wasn't as sour as this stuff. Without comment, Willem opened another bottle, filled my glass and went to the window, looking at his wristwatch.

How long would I have to listen to this? It was half past twelve, according to the vinyl wall clock that Willem bought thirty years ago, his only purchase from me ever. The clock was a consolation prize for himself because he couldn't afford the tellurion, based on an old design by Kepler, that he so desired. One afternoon after work a few weeks later, I took the tellurion to his house across the street as a gift. First I fixed it, and then I had to smuggle it down the stairs without my father noticing. With its naïve representation of the cosmos, it was really quite a valuable piece. Willem was ecstatic. He looked at me with sparkling eyes. I didn't want to stay for tea. At the door, he touched my hand before I could shove it into my coat pocket. Do let me thank you, he said. I left quickly, and for the next month I made up excuses not to work in the studio upstairs. By the time I next dared to take my perch there, he'd moved out. He left a short note under the shop's door: Dear Jacob, Come for a cup of tea with me at 108 Stadhouderskade, interesting view!

And here I was again, at yet another new address with an interesting view, and it wasn't tea, it was wine, as always. As in all Willem's previous homes that I'd visited over the years, the tellurion again took pride of place that afternoon in Wester-straat. It was set up on a half-moon table, next to the cane stand by the door. The ivory spheres of the earth and its moon on their matte metal arms, the sconce polished to its full copper-red sheen with a new candle inserted as the sun, the cogs at the base set to autumn – it was the only well-maintained item in Willem's mausoleum of crap.

When he saw me looking at it, he lit the candle, wound up the tellurion with its wing nut, and took the latch off the cog. The contraption came to life with a start, the planets in their orbits of light and shadow. Real sunlight shone into the room through the rustling beech branches, scattering sparkling discs of illumination across the writing table, the floor, the half-moon table, over the cheeks of the moon and the earth, and onto the wall behind them. I confess, Mevrouw, the gesture mollified me. A homage to our friendship, that's what I thought. When he was finished with his story, I'd tell him about the Hercules water clock I saw in Gaza, and how badly I'd missed him during the trip, as though I was in a dream with only half of myself. Would he feel the same, so hopeless and disoriented, if he had to write a story without me in the vicinity? We clinked our glasses and, at exactly five minutes to one, entered chapter two of "The Percussionist". Like children, I thought, holding hands on a path through the forest.

*

The percussionist was blinded by his infatuation with the young woman, Willem continued, sitting opposite me again at the writing table. The spellbound drummer moved about in the room, "swooning and wafting" as though he were swimming in prenatal fluid, his hands "stretched out like starfish before him, groping for the one he worshipped", his face awash with involuntary twitches. His lips never stopped moving, he was so full of declarations of love and sweet nothings. The girl watched him without a word.

For two whole weeks, Willem said, they never got out of bed. Only at nightfall would they go out to buy a baguette, liverwurst, cheese, apples, sour gherkins, herring and wine, all to be eaten and drunk from each other's mouths, naked before the open window. And then they'd fall back into bed to indulge and consume each other yet again. What could be heard of it in the courtyard, according to Willem, were sighs and groans and erratic breathing, interspersed with long monologues by the young builder, his voice distorted with passion. Not once did the girl speak. And in the corner, he writes here, stood the drum kit, gleaming and untouched. I quote: "The bass drum in its red formica mounting, a pomegranate on the verge of bursting open, the hi-hat with pursed lips like those of a priest before a sacrificial virgin."

Sighs and groans, erratic breathing? Was he meshugge enough to go and buy some sort of eavesdropping device to complement his binoculars? I asked.

No, Kippelstein, Willem said, everything could be heard quite clearly from across the courtyard, and the sounds came from him more than from her; she was a "Moira who loaded the young man with desire, as one loads a pianola with a roll of music".

Looking back, Mevrouw, I must say that I felt exactly the same that afternoon as the hours passed, as though something was being invested in me. Do I detect the same discomfort among you, dear listeners? You're probably thinking this isn't a suitable story for a eulogy. Do I have your permission to continue, Mevrouw? I know you knew him well: He always spoke of his sister Helena, who could see into his head like it was glass, but nonetheless reacted to his stories like a "dove driven out from under the awning by a song that someone begins singing indoors, only to be lured back later by the same music". Did he ever tell you this himself?

Willem lit a cigarette and looked out the window with the burning match in his hand, eyes screwed up, and only resumed when his fingertips began to singe, his gaze intense, his voice too high.

Do you know anything, even just from the books you've read, he asked suddenly, about the phenomenon known as "post-orgasmic dysphoria", referred to in the Middle Ages by the expression "omne animal post coitum triste"?

Could he explain it in layman's terms, and kindly refrain from using any more Latin, I asked, since not all of us had attended a goy gymnasium where one could study all the esoteric dimensions of eroticism.

Every little birdy feels cheated after mating, that's what it means, he said, but this young man, the drummer, felt much more than that. Had I, Jacob Kippelstein Junior, ever felt so utterly screwed?

I beg your pardon? I said.

Well, Willem said, have you not spent your entire life looking at the most expressionless faces on earth, namely those of clocks, and is this perhaps why you never show your feelings? Perhaps you've been infected by your profession?

Infected how? I asked.

Now, Willem said, slightly slurring, you know what I mean, you're always sitting with your fingers in the tabernacle of Time, but does she ever show any enjoyment? No, her face remains un-moved. And so does yours. You're a perfect match, you and your clock faces, but don't forget, it is time, the irreversibility of time itself, that compels us to dam her up in a story, in a piece of music, in a biography, a divine history, every piece with a start and a finish, every artwork a veil we hang over the unbearably senseless passing of minutes, centuries, generations.

Mevrouw Oldemarkt, I see you shaking your head, and in-deed that was my reaction too that afternoon. You couldn't take him seriously when he was like that, but I was feeling a bit rebellious. What do you know about my sorrow, Willem Olde-markt, storyteller? That's what I thought. You didn't want to go on holiday with me, the only holiday we would ever have had together, because apparently you had to move house urgently. This wasn't fiction, this was my life.

May I use this empty chair beside you, Mevrouw? I need to sit down for a moment.

Where was I?

I was discussing the lover's expressionless face. It was the im-movable visage of the girl that seemed to torment the young man, Willem told me. Every time he "mounted" her, he took her face in his hands and begged her to look at him, to say aloud that she loved him, to join him in his ecstasy, not abandon him in his rapture. But she just gazed at him with "Asian indifference". So the young man tried to free the words he so wanted to hear from her with a few firm thrusts, as though she were a pipe holding trapped air. But only his own tears were dislodged, and every time he reached a climax, he wailed: Hold my head! Hold my head! as though his brain was literally bursting from his skull, and he wanted his lover to "reassemble its loosened windings into two lobes, and then fit the plates and the cap of the cranium around them like a lab assistant constructing a model of a skull . . ."

At this point I could no longer suppress my frustration, and I finished Willem's sentence for him; it sounded more sarcastic than I meant it to: . . . and that she should then strap the builder's helmet onto this reconstructed skull, just to be sure.

That got his attention, and with a sad smile he said: It takes quite a lot of fiction, Jacob, to move *you*, and now, after more than thirty years, I've finally succeeded; maybe I should give *you* the chance to bring this story to completion.

Did he have some premonition, I wonder. I've never seen myself as a finisher, at best as a sparring partner. I specialised in time and he specialised in fiction. I was the immovable horizon for him to use for shadow-boxing. We were a good match, travelling companions you might say, me with an eye on the sun and him with an eye on the road; certainly a pair who could get some consolation and support from each other here on terra firma. After one of these sessions at Willem's, I could return to my daily grind with new energy, while he'd always invite me back a week later to listen to a revised version of the story, one now more tempered with respect for the reader.

A good story, Jacob, he often said, is "like an apple orchard that must be found in the thick fog of language". But can I find it alone? I need your help, dear listeners. Let's get cracking, we need to row him across the Styx in one piece.

*

Just when he thought it was the end of the saga, Willem continued, one night there was a change in the affaire in the percussionist's home, as the "beech released her mellowest sigh in the sultry summer air". It happened after a battle of love-making spanning several hours, the likes of which he'd never seen before, even though, as I well knew, he'd pretty much seen the Pope in a jacuzzi full of choirboys.

I'll try to piece together the description of this night of passion from these densely inscribed pages:

It was a corruption of the realm of the senses. The sweating bodies in the candlelight were like snakes in hell. If they let each other go it was only to bite and slap, before getting caught again in a carnage of arms and legs, with the walls and the sheets gradually becoming spattered with blood. Throughout the struggle, the young man clawed at his collarbones, moaning that he wanted to tear the skin from his body.

Did the drummer not understand, Willem asked, that to plead for love was asking too much? And could I, his dear friend, imagine something of the events in the room across the courtyard, and how it might end?

Perhaps he should have made a few audio recordings for me to go with this so-called love history, I said, then I might be better able to advise.

Kippelstein, fuck you! he bellowed, has there ever been a story from my pen that was not seated in real events?

I knew only too well of this real seat and all who'd sat in it. How many times had Willem not disappeared for weeks without explanation? You're nodding, Mevrouw Oldemarkt? You recognise this behaviour? I would always know when he was having a crush on someone new, and that he'd write it up as soon as it was over, and that I'd once again be called as his witness. Not to witness the infatuation, but to attest to the fantasy. Because nothing meaningful ever came from these so-called great loves of Willem's. The stories were all he retained. He held on to them for dear life. They were his real lovers, I only realise this now.

In an "upstroke of frustration", Willem told me, the percussionist finally tore himself away from the fight with his lover and fell upon his drum kit with sticks, fists, feet, as though he was trying to wrestle down an angel. Soon all the lights in the courtyard were on, the neighbours yelling "godverdomme" and "sodomieterop" and "bel de politie". The racket on the drums soon subsided, but the final thumps from the percussionist's home had a different tone, said Willem: The closing bars were like a conversation between two defeated voices, soft, compliant, accepting, tired.

Willem took two pestles from the mortar on his table and played me those closing beats of the fight on the tabletop. He played softly and with feeling, his head bent low over his hands. And remarkably, I could make out exactly what he was illustrating: question, answer, response, sigh.

After this, Willem said, the candles in the apartment behind the beech tree were blown out, and there was nothing more to be seen. All was quiet. Only the city echoed around the courtyard, like the sea in a shell.

*

Oh, Mevrouw Oldemarkt, you must know what it's like to be left behind. He was your only surviving relative, after your father's passing. He was my only friend. Now there is no one in my life to make such claims on me. Now I sit in his home for days, sorting out papers, and all I can hear is the buzz of the city in the courtyard. The grinding sounds of trams, the hissing water pipes, the ticking electricity meters, the creaking roof trusses, the comings and goings of people, laughing, talking; all the sounds of the city that we've grown old with. And in the background, the rustling beech outside the window, where the leaves are no longer in concert, but loosen from the branches and flutter down to where they'll moulder in the wintry silence.

Does someone have a handkerchief for me? Thank you, Mevrouw. You're nodding. Would you like to hear the rest of it?

On the morning after that nocturnal outburst, according to Willem, everything between the lovers was different. Or rather, the young man's attitude towards the girl, the way he looked at her, was different. After making love, he'd put his head on her chest and they'd lie together like that for hours, as though under the spell of something, something that now belonged to him and no longer to her. There was no sign of the feverish, pleading expression of before, the desperate overdependence, his urgent fixation on her face. This had been replaced by something that Willem could only call "sovereignty".

Jesus, Willem, the percussionist as little prince, I said. Why can't you stick with a simple construction worker, at peace with the situation? Why does something extraordinary always materialise in front of you? A person much more glamorous than he really is?

You don't want to understand, Jacob, he said. It's a form of compensation. All my readers can recognise themselves in it. Why don't you?

Making art is the only reliable form of self-consolation, and he realised this, said Willem, when the young man got up one day after lying with his head on the girl's chest for a long while, walked over to his drum kit and started tapping out a tom-tom rhythm on the middle drum. Lub-dub, lub-dub – it was *her heartbeat*, the heartbeat we all have, Jacob, the one you can feel by pressing your fingers to your clavicle.

He patted the beat on the table for me with the palm and fingers of his right hand. Loss shouldn't be scorned, he said, it is the fountain in which sovereigns bathe. It is the source of all we call beauty. Beauty as consolation.

I want to present this in the author's own words, with your permission, Mevrouw Oldemarkt, if I may have a few more minutes. I'll read you a paragraph marked "Revise", meaning Willem wanted to retain something from it in the next version.

And so, because she never talked, he turned into her eavesdropper, catching all her ins and outs. He studied her sounds without her noticing. He listened to the resonance in her neck as she brushed her hair in the mirror, he heard her small, tawny wrist as she stirred her coffee at breakfast, he hearkened to her jawbone as she bit into a bread crust, and listened to her belly grumbling some hours later. The chime of her ankle bracelets, her footsteps on the stairs, like knocking on a wooden temple fish going up, the descent like beating a tambourine, the musical scales of her laugh, the colours of her sighs, her itsy-bitsy sips as she drank water from the tap, the tensing of her kneecaps as she bent to tie her thongs, her feather-duster breaths as she slept. His ear was caught by all of this, he recorded every percussive thing that came from her, yes, even the quaking grass of her dreams filled his imagination, her desire like the small fugue of a lark over a field of ripened wheat. Her very skin resounded under his caress, her hips thrumming like harps.

The next paragraph is also still legible, although it has been struck through; I shall read it to you to illustrate how every Oldemarkt story was built on "night soil", as he put it.

At the door to the toilet he listened as she peed, yes, her stools he pursued, her farts and her soft groans, plumpest lady turds plopping into the bowl, and one morning he held a thin film of foil under her chin as she cried, tracking the spattering tears while softly copying her sorrowful sobs in his throat and slyly drumming out the sound of the drops on the headboard; every cough was noted in the book he kept beside their bed. Her voice baffled him: After he had stopped begging for vows, she started murmuring like a stream, always on the verge of song, and marbling it all with words from her own language that he asked her to repeat slowly, the little explosions on both sides of the vowels, the wordflesh pure fruit; and he had a godly nose for the aroma, connoisseur of a made-up thing. He noted the chatter of her poppy chin, his face turned to hers beatifically, tapping a finger on her knee as if she were a drum he was teasing before the big bang; until she realised that despite his intense attention he couldn't remember a thing she'd said, and slapped his face – smack! He noted this on his stave, as percussion for hand and human cheek.

The young man was a "sly knight", according to Willem. With one hand he'd feed his lover strawberries; with the other he wrote her down. Sometimes he played her sketches from his composition on the drums, saying: It's you, it's all for you, I dedicate this to you. But she wasn't so easily fooled. It's not about *me*. You're in love with your music, she said.

And then, two days later, almost two months after she'd first stepped into his life and at a critical point in his notation of her corporeal music – she ran off. And all at once, with summer still glinting in the beech, the young man was alone, not only in his bed but also in his composition, without a model, without material, without a listener, utterly dry-docked.

*

Why is everyone getting up? Where are we going? Did you say something, Mevrouw? No, of course we weren't sober! Who could stay dry with such Quatsch on a weekday? Boruch and Zoruch and the malech hamoves? No, there was no more wine. It was a flask of jenever. Willem took it out at four and poured us a drink in the glasses I'd given him for his fiftieth birthday. Woodstock glass, hand-engraved spiral around the ball. A toast in an old man's hand, lit up by the gleam of leaves and jenever. L'Chayim! I cried, to "The Percussionist"!

And . . . oh? Excuse me, who is taking me by the elbow? Am I being escorted off? Through the hatch to heaven that opens up behind me? Are we going to the grave now? Under umbrellas? To think, you can't even order nice weather over your own god-damned tomb.

No, I don't need a wheelchair, Mevrouw, I can walk perfectly well, thank you, here behind the coffin, the only square box anyone could ever package Willem in. Ausgeputzt in Essig und Honig. Will nobody hold my hands in the air so that time stands still? Must I hold them up myself, like autumn's conductor? Look, the leaves on the coffin, hearts on the dusky wood. Under his own beech I would've buried him, in his own courtyard. Über sein Bett erhebt sich ein Baum.

How can you let someone leave like this, and how can you leave someone behind, so alone? Abandoned, with such a mess on their hands? That's what I asked Willem that afternoon, Mevrouw, when he made the percussionist's girlfriend disappear just like that.

How else would there be a story, my friend? he said. If nobody goes away and nobody's left behind, if everyone stayed home cosily cleaning up the mess, the good Lord above could never have inspired his prophets to write the Holy Book.

*

You see where this is going? Please hold my hat over the papers, Mevrouw, so that this precious manuscript does not get wet. May I read you a fragment?

He expanded his drum kit with everything that might be played to represent his departed lover. He converted his whole room into a percussion installation, tubes, glasses, seeds, shells, all hung on strings criss-crossing the room, and every day he would climb up to touch each one softly in turn, as though trying to reach her, she who had sailed over the horizon; to voyage once more to that island where love is eternal, a land of summer nights, and he the boatman in the crow's nest of yearning.

Please hold my papers, like this, under the umbrella, Mevrouw, let me read another passage:

How could he play her dark hair? With a lithophone of slate bars brushed with pieces of lead? And the way she stretched after waking up? With a plectrum over a bicycle wheel turning fast and then slow? And her smile as she walked through the door – the thumb on the sweet spot of the Hang?

Do you know what a Hang is, Mevrouw? I didn't know either, until Willem showed me an image of one in his file one afternoon. An esoteric instrument, hand-made by a company in Switzerland. There were hundreds of pictures of percussion instruments in his collection.

You're looking at me like I'm crazy, Mevrouw, but there's a surprise in store for you, just like there was one for me. I didn't realise where it all was going that afternoon as Willem, with growing excitement, told me his story. Apparently, the young man had spent all his money on a set of Zildjian cymbals as well as drumsticks and brushes. Each day Willem watched as the drummer came home with new treasures. He tuned three big toms and two pedal basses, plus five piccolo toms, so he could play an ostinato to carry the tone along with the other beats. He'd refined his technique to a point where each of his four limbs could be used interchangeably and independently in four different rhythms, and he could speed up and syncopate each one on its own. He'd broken down his entire body and rebuilt it in order to "become a lover who would never fail again".

Is this a child's spade you've given me, Mevrouw? A clump of wet cat litter to plop down onto the lid? Oh, to end it all with such a sparse little sound! Oh Oldemarkt, how I wish for you a hammer-toned casket with a clanging edge onto which we could throw pebbles, or imagine under every tombstone a musician, violins, clarinets, with you at the furnace on pitch-black kettle drums. The terrible kitchen! With roses and cannons!

Mein Lieber, dieser schwere Augenblick! Shall I chuck your binoculars into the hole? Your sister's hung them back around my neck. You're not allowed to spy on your own maggots. There goes your hat! They're pulling me away by my sleeves, I see my shoes, I taste my snot, they're wiping my upper lip. Powder, mothballs and peppermint of your reading public. Hands keep me from the edge. Fluttering against my chest, fingers of the accordion, cheeks of the baritone, the dreadlocks of the didgeridoo, all of them here for your farewell.

So, is that it then, Mevrouw – after an entire life, this meagre farewell? Shuffling past his grave with a spadeful of Proud Cat, and now we go back? To a reception with canapés?

How far was I with the story? Willem, with your story that I must finish telling? On this afternoon where you're hanging in the straps, soon to descend and be covered up, hopefully with some more honest earth?

You're prodding my back, Mevrouw? You're steering me by the

elbow? Through this door? To this white table? Onto this plastic chair?

Yes, thank you, fill my glass. Why are they giving me such strange looks, haven't they ever seen a beetle on its back? A graveful of guitars, one old carp in the weir of remembrance?

*

Nice and cosy here at the table, isn't it? Better than that chapel, with its air so thick with lilies. The Sister to my right, the Publisher to my left. Two people laughing over there – do you think they want to hear the rest, Mevrouw? Cheers! May we live respected and die regretted. Who's even listening to the tick-tock man mumbling into his coat?

Do you want to know how the rest of the day went? A rolling pin, dear fellow diners, Willem put a rolling pin into my one hand that afternoon in Westerstraat, and a bicycle spoke in the other. Then he sat down opposite me with a cake tin on his lap.

Now we will figure it out together, Jacob, he said, by God I don't know how this story about the percussionist must end.

Why do you always have to make it so difficult? I asked. Just let the girl come back. A good chat with her bricklayer. A walk through the zoo, noodles at the Chinese. Pais en vree. Amen!

Philistine! Willem roared. Who would guess that your forefathers walked through the desert following a column of fire!

Nudnik! I thundered back. The Holy Scripture was inspired, not thought up by some dybbuk!

Nudnik, that's what my father used to call him, Mevrouw, and dybbuk, when he came into the shop. That was thirty years ago, when he lived across the way, on the second floor. My father had no time for customers who just browsed without buying anything. He always came up the stairs to my studio to chivvy me. Come down and get this nudnik, Jacob, he's wasting my time.

Back then, as you well know, Mevrouw, Oldemarkt was not yet well known, not even published. Always dressed in a white shirt and tweed jacket with leather patches on the elbows, a tie – not a façade behind which you'd suspect a voyeur to be hiding. I'd take him upstairs to get him out of my father's way, and he'd spend the entire afternoon perched on a bar stool next to my workbench, watching as I made something.

Your clocks, Mister Kippelstein, he'd say, are works of art. You sit here hour after hour repairing them, but as soon as they're filled with ticking, they're less convincing. Their enamelled faces, their cogs of copper and their silver mountings, their shoulders of cherrywood, these are the things that count, not their function of measuring out fleeting moments. Tick tock tick, what's there to experience? Come, take off your glasses, put down your pliers, come have a cup of tea with me across the road.

Across the road, indeed! Where I saw him spying on me every morning! The binoculars pressed to his face for hours at a time at his window, like a property speculator! For weeks I sat with my hands frozen on my worktable, too scared to put down my magnifying glass or to look up. I felt like a still life. And he stood there equally still, the binoculars pressed to his eyes, now and then lowering them to polish the lenses. What did he see in me? Me, small Yiddish clockmaker, with kippah and hook nose, a caricature from some children's book? And now here he was, standing in my shop as if butter wouldn't melt in his mouth, inviting me over! For a cup of tea! What did he want from me?

For all of thirty years, Mevrouw, I tried to understand, by my lights. Always listening to his stories, struggling through his Black Pages with him, when he worked for weeks at a time in his brown shirt. I took him kreplach and blintzen from the kosher delicatessen, now and then I took a bag of his dirty clothes to the laundry, sometimes I tackled the kitchen and washed his dishes.

Until that afternoon in Westerstraat, when I finally understood that he just wanted to play, to play with me just once, Mevrouw, if that's the word, to play. He wanted to teach me this. Why was I so slow on the uptake?

Nudnik, knick-knack, dybbuk, wake up! Willem called, and tapped the cake tin with a teaspoon. I pointed my rolling pin at the wall clock. It's getting late, I should get going, I said, and started putting on my shoes. He protested. Your whole life you've played the repairer of clockwork, he said, and now you want to run off when finally something happens that makes time fly!

Call your beekeeper, Meister Schriftsteller, phone your damn organist or one of your other youthful sweethearts. I shall listen, I shall read, but I shall not be an actor in your theatre.

Strong words indeed, Mevrouw, but we were used to each other after thirty years. Was there a challenge in his eye? It was the same look he'd had that afternoon when I gave him the tellurion, when I ran down the stairs, when he said he didn't want to die alone one day. Well, Mevrouw, for better or for worse, I'd made him my friend and kept him for thirty years, watching his lovers come and go. I was the one who had to help with the percussionist, just like I'd had to help with all of them, with the road builder, the conductor, the cantor; I had to drag them from the mud and stand them upright. All the monumental paramours! How did he put it? The calibre of the lover can only be measured by the glow of the beloved.

Yes, and then it started. And yes, thank you, Mevrouw, I'll have another meatball. And yes, you may refill my glass. How does the Ecclesiast put it? Eat, drink, make it stink . . . With the spoon on the pan, he started tapping out a rhythm. I had to beat a counter-rhythm, he said, with the bicycle spoke on a tin plate, and thump out the bassline on the table leg with my rolling pin. He hit the mobiles with a rolled-up newspaper, lit the fuses of the firecrackers.

Oh, sweet spinning tops of reconstructed time! he cried, with the blue smoke wafting around him. Spirals of reminiscence! Let your stories ring out! A teaspoon thrown away on a street corner! A bell from some lonely person's parakeet, a pebble, a twig, a firecracker from a Chinese shop on the Zeedijk, all these fragments that have washed up on my shores.

He stopped the mobiles and set them spinning in the opposite direction, with a stone-and-steel tinkle. He rowed his hands through the hanging rubbish. Listen to the time, Jacob, he called. We're making it *thick*, we're making *butter*, we are cheesemakers in the whey of seconds!

The whole time he was urging me on, tapping my chair leg with his walking stick. He put a flyswatter in my hand and kicked a cardboard box across the length of the room towards me.

For God's sake, Jacob! Get moving! Imagine you're doing something that gives you pleasure! Like wanking, or praying . . . I have no idea what you do to occupy yourself!

Just look at that guy's mouth hanging open, Mevrouw, his cheeks stuffed full of finger food. Does he find my story so shocking, or did he perhaps experience a similar experiment with Willem? On a different afternoon, at a different address, with different devices? Is this why they're staring at me like that? The whale-caller? The winemaker? Shall I look at them through your binoculars, Willem? They stare at me, do you see, Mevrouw – the clockmaker who's lost the plot at his friend's funeral. Well, shall I tell them how it all fits together? I've read them all this past week in that necrotic apartment on Westerstraat, Mevrouw, each and every one of the stories, except the one at the very bottom of the last box. He put that one there especially for me, the sly old fox.

Let me stand up straight, let me lay my serviette beside my

plate and lift my glass once more. Tonight at your table, for the
rest of your evenings at table, my friends, you can toast him. With
a knife against a plate, a fork tapping a glass, a small percussion
that rises above the hum of the city, up into the stars, caught by
the cherubs to jazz up their chanting.

Meanwhile, it was a quarter to five there on Westerstraat,
Mevrouw. I clenched the ruler between my teeth, like this, like
I'm doing now with my knife, and tapped the edge of the table
in three-quarter time, my one foot in a cha-cha-cha, the other
in a tango. And it was actually starting to sound like something.
Willem strummed a piece of fishing line with a toothbrush, the
room shook with our laughter; one would pick up a pipe or a slat
of wood that the other had dropped and play on, on the china on
the kitchen shelves – we smashed the lot to smithereens, the school
bell and the chamber pot, the walking stick against the door.

*Em*phasis, Willem thundered amidst it all, I want *em*phasis
in the paradiddle! A bull's-eye in the spark gap! He winked at
me, the moment anticipated, his head bobbing in time with the
rhythms and counter-rhythms until he shattered two glasses one
after the other in the hearth, against the beat. The appetisers,
that's what he called it, to import the vibration into the grain,
and then he tackled the mirror above the fireplace with a poker
and unleashed a waterfall of shards. The whole place was shaking.
And then he kicked over all three pyramids of olive-oil tins, and
finally grabbed the jenever flask by its neck for a big bang in the
fireplace. Up and down the chimney it rang, an apartment with an

echo chamber, with a glacier in the smoke pipe, the only canalside home in the city with such an auditory profile, the only one in the whole world, a first in the history of percussive improvisation, and beneath it all, the fine pedal point of the tellurion, ticking away on the half-moon table.

Rodika and Dodika! Willem called, play the big harmonica! And then we started dancing round and round, clapping our hands, wilder and wilder, with things falling and breaking all about us. Saladin, Willem called, come into my arms and spin into heaven with me!

Saladin? Do you know the reference, Mevrouw? You're shaking your head. You think I'm crazy? Saladin was a friend of Rumi's, I looked it up in the library; for the rest of my life I will be looking up the things that Willem mentioned that afternoon.

Well, better an idiot than an idol. Eventually someone started hammering on the door, the phone rang. What pokketeringherrie is this, what a sifkutkoleregekrys! Willem opened the door and I answered the phone. What in God's name was going on, they wanted to know. The Resurrection! Willem called at the door. The last trumpet, I whispered into the mouthpiece. Together we leaned out the courtyard window, me with a carpet beater on a frying pan and Willem with a nonsense poem and a castanet. Here, let me read it to you, it's in a footnote in the Black Pages.

Huakit thi mirammiti lili zimen nibni
Huec ucakit hi mirammiti vargia ibnie

Biddilihe inte il miken illi yeutihe
Min ibidil il miken ibidil i ventura!

*

We bellowed as we collapsed onto the couch, mirror shards all over the floor. We shook hands, four hands in a cross like children, Mevrouw, like children playing oranges and lemons.

No more of this loneliness, Jacob, he whispered to me. I have written myself a procession, road signs for my sultanless soul going *up* these ramshackle stairs, to build a new house.

What did he mean, Mevrouw? The Oldemarkt Procession? It does sound better than this march of owls past his hole that we've just witnessed. The cupbearer, the baker, kings in a dream with bells on their toes, his progeny.

It's going well with "The Percussionist", Jacob, Willem whispered to me, you've helped me immensely, all my life you've helped me, with every kind of work I've started: with window washing, with playing the harp, with street paving. I must rest now, the ending will write itself, the build-up was good, I thank you from my heart of hearts. You've been my only friend. Do not put away the bow, I am your arrow with four feathers. Heaven, earth, god and man.

And then he placed his hand on my leg, Mevrouw, I can tell you this, and I put my hand over his, held it there for some time, on Willem's small, dry, bony hand. It was the first time that I'd ever held hands with anyone. So small it felt, small and shrinking, and I thought: I loved you and I always longed for you, because you were always somewhere else.

He sank back against the back rest, closed his eyes. So pale, I thought, his face so gaunt; der arme Bub, that he suffers so for his work. I put his hand back in his lap and squeezed it, but he didn't squeeze back.

How long did I stay with him on the couch there in the growing gloom, with the floor covered in instruments from our concert?

Nobody, I thought, who stumbled upon this scene would ever understand what had happened here, ball bearings in the bread bin, a bicycle spoke in a mobile, a walking stick in the warming drawer, jenever in the fireplace. And on the half-moon table the tellurion, the candle's flame lighting up the moon and the earth in their orbits, even more brightly as it had grown dark. The painted plates at its base ticking over from l'automne to l'hiver, the darkened face of the sun.

Can you understand why I had to share this with you? Me, someone who felt, through the fibres of his flannel trousers and through his rumpled skin and through his old-man's flesh, a warmth spreading in his bones? And who wasn't afraid? For the first time in his life, was not afraid of the closeness of another person?

Why are you looking away, Mevrouw? Here, have the serviette.

The lights in the courtyard were turned on, it was after six already, but I lingered. I sat down in Willem's chair at his writing table and took in his view, the courtyard, the rustling beech. And all at once, right in front of me I saw it, a hole in the leaves! I took the binoculars and peered through the opening, right into the percussionist's room: a bed, a table and chair, one picture hanging on the wall. Clearly a young man's home. Everything neat, the windows closed, the bed made, no clothes on the chair. The home of someone on a summer holiday. And, yes, no sign of a drum kit in red formica mountings, not a cymbal in sight!

There on the desk was Willem's manuscript, this one I'm holding in my hand now. I paged through it until I reached the last heading: "First Design for an Ending".

May I read it to you? To this handful of last guests, with your permission, Mevrouw? Do you have just a few more minutes? Soon everyone can leave into the perfectly ordinary night in their perfectly ordinary coats, with an everyday goodbye, holding the door for each other and stepping out onto the predictable street, stopping for a moment on the pavement before they head up the street, to the tram, the bus, the train.

*

The percussionist's composition was not working. Pulverised by his struggles, he sank down and lay among the clappers and sticks, in the nest of nylon strings from the broken floor guitar, and covered his head.

One morning he woke up and knew what he had to do. He loaded all the percussion instruments onto a carrier bike and transported them to the dump, everything except his old drum kit and the score of his unfinished composition. On his return, he swept the floor and cleaned the drums. And once the kit was nice and shiny again, screws polished and pedal repaired and toms dusted, he took his score and one by one tore the sheets into tiny pieces, and let them drift down onto the clean surfaces.

Was it just out of habit that he tilted his head to listen to those densely inscribed pieces of paper falling onto the cymbal? Lighter than tears the sound was, finer than snowflakes, more tender than the morning mist, the sound of stars reflecting in a puddle, the soft thumps of moths against a lantern. He closed his eyes and tore up a thousand and one sheets of paper and let the small pieces flutter down, and he listened.

And guided by this fluttering of shreds, he started to play the song of his loss, without hesitation, softly and uninterrupted, as though the score was written in his heart. A masterwork that ended as it started, with four soft beats. And when he was finished he sobbed bitterly, for a summer that was over and a composition he would never repeat, and a lover he'd remember to the end of his days.

*

It was almost dark by the time I finished reading the ending. Willem was fast asleep on the couch. He seemed so small, with his eyelids wrinkled together. The air was turning chilly outside. I went to his bedroom to fetch a blanket. I stood for a while in that somewhat musty bedroom, the bedding turned back at the corner, just enough for him to crawl out in the morning and back in at night, a hollow in the mattress that cupped his body. The closet was open and I could see how little clothing he owned. The hat I'd given him when he started going bald at forty was on a hook beside the bed – I put it on when I feel like dreaming, he once told me, and I want to be wearing it when you bury me. There was a frayed shaving brush on the washbasin, stacks of books on the floor. Boxes of manuscripts with lists of titles on the lids.

I pulled the bedspread off the bed and brought it into the living room to cover him. So peacefully exhausted he was, a small smile on his face as though to say: "Done reading at my table in the twilight, Tweedledum? Don't think I don't know what you've been doing. And now you're going to look through my binoculars just one more time at what's going on over there, this I know as well."

I pulled the bedspread up to his chin and kissed his forehead.

Are they turning off the lights? Are you leading me outside? Are they closing for the night? Do you still want to hear the ending, Mevrouw?

I looked through the binoculars. I saw someone entering the room on the far side of the courtyard, a young man in his twenties with a backpack and a blue gym bag from the Magic Bus. He was tanned and the sun had bleached his blond hair, and there was a red bandana around his neck. He took the backpack off and opened the windows, lit a cigarette and smoked it by the window, relaxing and gazing at nothing. An attractive boy, just as in Willem's story, an Ariel with one gold earring. And then he pulled up the chair and took the picture down from the wall. It was a rock-band poster, with big red letters across the top: *The Grateful Dead*. And at the bottom was the name of the soloist in the spotlight, Mickey Hart, the drummer. The young man opened his backpack and pulled out a cardboard tube containing another poster, unrolled it, and climbed onto the chair again to hang it, exactly over the white square occupied until moments ago by the Grateful Dead drummer.

You want to know what was on the new poster, Mevrouw? Are you getting onto the tram with me? Could you please stamp my ticket?

It was a beach in Greece: a strip of black sand, a cleft of azure sea, a sunny day. And in big white letters: *Atlantis – Sunken City*.

Over the Amstel in the tram. I haven't done this in some time. I know a painter who lives in a houseboat further upstream, Mevrouw, who's been painting the same square of river his whole life. *The River Below*, that's what he calls each and every canvas.

You realise now what happened to Willem, Mevrouw? Slowly it dawned on me, as I sat there in his chair looking at the perfectly ordinary young man who'd just returned from a holiday in Greece, returned to his perfectly ordinary room with its perfectly ordinary poster of a pop star on the wall. Willem had fallen in love with this young neighbour at the start of summer, and suddenly the beautiful boy had left to go on holiday. And thus ended the spying. And to compensate, he'd made up a story.

You see: Not through binoculars but through his imagination, that's how he'd filled that empty room with a percussive extravaganza, a mushroom cloud of fabrications based on longing. A poster of a drum kit was all the inspiration he needed.

And *this* story, Mevrouw, is what he told his friend on the last day of his life.

Truth is stranger than fiction, indeed.

Only when I got home did I realise I'd taken the wrong coat from the rack. The next evening I went back to fetch my own coat. I found him there on the couch, just as I'd left him.

Tell you what, come with me to the Spiegelgracht? It can't do any harm. We've seen the worst, haven't we? I have cold vodka and green olives. I could show you my most beautiful clocks, the Comtoises, the Bornholms. And then you can tell me about your childhood. Willem never wanted to speak about his mother, only his father, who'd taught him to name the clouds.

You're crying? With your head on my chest in the tram? Let me put my arm around you.

What did you say?

A bit louder, please?

That we shall feel lonely more often now? You and I?

Oh, what is "alone" anyway, I'm still here and so are you. You remind me of my mother. I still smell her last bottle of perfume every single day. My father kept it in his desk drawer and I took it when he passed away; now it's in my own drawer. Chanel No. 5. Maybe I should give it to you. What are we to each other, what more than the guardians of melancholic aromas?

The stars shine on us. I am the half-moon, as Rumi says, hung above the gate to the festival. And what shall we call this new kind of looking-tram in which we now travel the city? Where people sit still and pour their gazes over us like light, like answers?

You want to know more about me?

Only one person could inform you, Mevrouw, and we buried him today. But I have a suggestion. Actually, it's a favour I want to ask. I found a special manuscript at the bottom of a box in Willem's room this morning, the very last box I unpacked. The manuscript at the bottom, under all the incomplete ones, under "The Snow Sleeper", under "The Swan Whisperer", there in an envelope, thirty-six "White Pages". I dared not read it: the first story he ever finished, thirty years ago, and which was never published.

Will you please read it, carefully, on a chair under my reading lamp in the studio, while I pour us some vodka and wind up the old clocks for you?

And then, afterwards, would you tell me what it says?

Just the short version, please?

Of "The Clockmaker"?   *Jacob*

The Snow Sleeper

A Field Report

Conversation

Ordinary people are peculiar too:
Watch the vagrant in their eyes
Who sneaks away while they are talking with you
Into some black wood behind the skull,
Following un-, or other, realities,
Fishing for shadows in a pool.

But sometimes the vagrant comes the other way
Out of their eyes and into yours
Having mistaken you perhaps for yesterday
Or for tomorrow night, a wood in which
He may pick up among the pine-needles and burrs
The lost purse, the dropped stitch.

Vagrancy however is forbidden; ordinary men
Soon come back to normal, look you straight
In the eyes as if to say 'It will not happen again',
Put up a barrage of common sense to baulk
Intimacy but by mistake interpolate
Swear-words like roses in their talk.

(Louis MacNeice)

Helena Oldemarkt
43 Lauriergracht
1016 RT Amsterdam

18 October 2008

The Director
Landelike Onderzoeksteam Onbehuisden
Vrije Universiteit
Amsterdam

Dear Professor Sprinkhuizen,

Kindly refer to interview with vagrant: Dienst Onderzoek en Statistiek. Amsterdam 2008.

After numerous attempts to contact you telephonically – your secretary says that you are in the field monitoring fieldworkers at the moment – I am taking the liberty of writing to you.

You will find attached selections from an edited transcription of an interview, if this is the correct term, that I conducted on the night of 10 July 2008 with someone who shall be referred to as "the snow sleeper", for want of a clearer identification. The conversation took place under the auspices of the annual census of vagrants of the Dienst Onderzoek en Statistiek in Amsterdam, where I have been a volunteer for some years now, since the death of my father. The work forms part of my doctoral studies on vagrants in the urban context, supervised by your colleague Dr Gottlieb van Doorn, Instituut voor Nieuw Sociologisch Onderzoek, Utrecht. A framed copy of the poem by MacNeice I quoted hangs above his desk.

I would like to start off by declaring my interest – I volunteer to work with the disadvantaged as a form of consolation. My father was itinerant in the last years of his life, before I had him institutionalised. And now, by some strange stroke of fate, it seems my turn to be lost. Promoted from fieldworker to vagabond in the blink of an eye.

As you will see in my transcript, as far as I could, I adhered to the manual and the questionnaire you developed for the investigation. Although I have gathered the required information, I have never been confronted in this way, not once in all my years of interviewing the homeless.

I realise that you are first and foremost a statistician, and that as compiler and rural coordinator of the survey you have very little to do with qualitative research. Recommendations to the State regarding the homeless must be based on hard facts. Nonetheless, I thought it wise to involve you in the substance and process of this particular case. You see, it concerns, among other things, a potentially serious crime, committed, according to the subject, in the "Witte Hartensteeg" in Amsterdam in the winter of 2007/08. However, closer investigation shows that there is no alley by this name in Amsterdam. Going by his directions, the place he refers to is the Schapenburgerpad, an unpaved informal alleyway behind P.C. Hooftstraat.

To date I have informed neither the local branch of the Dienst O&S nor the police of this case, a dereliction which may be seen as incriminating in the judicial sense. However, my more immediate concern is that the subject may have started stalking me since the interview. He knows who I am, and could easily have looked up my address in the telephone directory. I have not caught him in the act thus far. I would go so far as to say that the eyes I feel upon me are not those of someone with malicious intent, but rather those of a "performer", as he calls himself, who wants to try his luck, although what he is after I would not know. I am a single middle-aged woman, or at least that is how I have seen myself until recently. Right now, I do not dare go outside without dressing like a bag lady myself. I feel I need to be careful entering my own home. He is the kind who, like a shadow (a melody? an aroma?), will slip past and let himself in as soon as you turn your back.

For three months, I have been wandering, in a state of what I can only call "heightened consciousness", past all the migrant accommodation and night shelters of HVO-Querido, the Leger des Heils and the beneficiaries of the Stoelenproject, without seeing a trace of him. At night I sit in the café of the Volksverbond on Haarlemmerstraat and question those who come in, but to no avail. I keep expecting him to appear at any moment. I also spend several hours daily at the Schapenburgerpad, next to the tangible remains of his winter residence, but he has never returned.

What will I do if I run into him one day? If he presented himself to me? Would I recognise him? How would we speak to each other? Would we keep fishing for shadows, or would we dare come closer this time? How will I pass my days if I can no longer search for him (his gestures, his sound, his impossible stories), if I can no longer expect to find him?

I hope that you can advise me in this dubious case of transference between caregiver and the incapacitated, drawing on your specialised knowledge and wide experience. I trust that you will not become ensnared in the same web of conjecture, false references and trickery that I have fallen prey to. It is quite enough if *one* participant in this survey has fallen under the spell of a mirage from the realm of chance.

Yours sincerely
Helena Oldemarkt (fieldworker, Dienst Onderzoek en Statistiek, Amsterdam, 2008)

Employee number: MW 112358
Telephone (home): 020 6365538
Mobile: 0642260320

PS
Due to an inexplicable problem with my recording equipment, my own voice has disappeared from the tapes. Therefore, there is no transcription of my own contribution to the conversation.

As a result, I have had to fill in the words of the subject as best I could wherever his story became incoherent or his pronunciation unclear. Due to the unfortunate fact that the three tapes I received from the Dienst O&S ran out, I could not record the tirade that formed his farewell to me. Perhaps the outburst was a defence against our mutual shyness. For your perusal, I include running memoranda of my observations and considerations throughout this conversation. Also included are insights I arrived at in the subsequent months, when I listened to the recordings again.

Transcription: The Snow Sleeper
Interview text Ams C 37, 10 July 2008
Memoranda 11 July – 19 October 2009

Memo 1

My typical Friday night excursion, hobo-spotting, equipment in a satchel over my shoulder, somewhat unwilling to be outside because I'd been getting on with writing a chapter on the depersonalisation of the vagrant in society. I find the subject at the rosarium in the Vondelpark, on a bench under one of the elm trees. He's in his early sixties, with waves of silver hair and greenish-brown eyes, unshaven, with the typical sunburn of a drifter who has long been exposed to the elements. I am triggered by unusual cadences, a weird kind of glossolalia, stirring the air in the rose garden. (Don't I always prick up my ears in the city for unusual sounds? A habit from my rural youth, inherited from my father. You could *hear* it when something was amiss in the countryside where I grew up.)

At his feet, a plastic bag of food and a flask he drinks from now and then. His right shoe is on his foot, the other is placed in front of him as a begging bowl. Also, a faded pair of jeans, a blue golf cap and a brand-new white windbreaker with an advert for Golden Tulip on the back, for a week's accommodation in a luxury suite (cf. "Zwervers als wandelende reclameborden", *de Volkskrant*, 12 August 2008, page 4). It's around eight, and he's on a roll. When he notices the microphone in my hand, he lifts his cap and winks, like he's been expecting me. The passers-by are mostly seniors, autochthones out on an evening stroll (the younger ones have vacant expressions and wear earphones; they can't hear anything over the white noise in their own heads). The song below is the first piece during which I could get close enough to record. He announces the performance as an "overture" and bows to the audience. A rather literary text, I must say, but set to the tune of a tear-jerker. My first note on my clipboard: a man who dares to disagree with himself.

Transcription: Recording Snow Sleeper, tape index 1-3

Oh, I am but the sound in a shell
hiding sorrow in my grooves
a glow-worm in kitchen soot
mumbling softly during church

And no one peering in can see
who I, if the stars so will, must be
three demons inside me reading still
the black book of the peregrine

Summered in a hall of mirrors
wintered in a dome of snow
a park bench or a narrow alley
my endless farces just for you

Who look for me, a risk do take
who find me, all are blind to see
from housetop snow to beechwood bronze
the spirits of words fall in my wake

Memo 2

The above is presented according to the conventions of a lieder performance. He assumes a grandiose pose in the late light, nods at me as if I am his accompanist. An imposing figure. In the play of sunlight and shadows, his hair seems alive, a new animal, as my late father would have said. Who is this man? Again, the conspiratorial eye contact. Should I leave, I wonder – but I'm already almost his stage hand. What is this master's craft, his jaw like a pike's, his mouth like a tulip? A surprisingly true baritone, in any case. Afterwards, general acclaim, small change clattering into his shoe, and the crowd calls out for more. I try to get closer with my recorder. I notice that his shoes carry the mark of Mercurius.

Transcription: Recording Snow Sleeper, tape index 4

Look who's throwing something into the heel of the month of August! Silver under the heel wing!

No, godalmighty, this deserves more, kind sir, than your coppers, do you think I'm a monkey ringing cheap bells? All morning long I've been sitting here under the beech, a fox fabricating for you an evening song in the Vondelpark, and you can't reach deeper into your pouch than for a nail?

*And motherofjesus what kind of a pieremachochel have we here,
holding her microphone to my nose as though it's a carnation of blue
velvet? A skivvy from the Salvation Army? Where is the hat of god's
own air hostess? If I were you, I wouldn't be watching a clochard in a
park on a summer's evening like this, you might just catch something
nasty in the cunt, parlez-vous français? Gift me with a silverling
then, s'il vous plaît, and I will tell you of a winter without equal.*

Memo 3

The atmosphere under the tree in the sultry summer air makes
my skin tingle. There's just a thin wall between us, I think. His
tone and approach remind me of my father, that provocation
of the listener. Building a customer base, he always used to call
it when he lured us to his chair with a song or a little rhyme,
especially me. I had to be tricked into it, wary as I was. But with
"The branch in the tree and the tree in the woods and the green
grass grew all around", he could always get me out from under
my rock.

I show the vagrant my identification card from the Dienst
O&S. He spells my name out carefully, taps his temple with
a finger. I ask if I may conduct an interview with him, carefully
emphasising that there will be no compensation. I read him the
confidentiality agreement. Nothing he says will be used in any
way outside the scope of this investigation, and his identity will
be protected. We both sign it, his signature a flamboyant scrawl.
The bystanders start to leave, a few linger in earshot. He looks me

up and down as I explain my mission. An unusual dizziness takes hold of me, like when I rode on the back of my father's bicycle through a poplar grove, long shadows flickering on my eyelids.

Transcription: Recording Snow Sleeper, tape index 5

Oh, she serenades me so lovingly in the crepuscule of the park, the last lark. Does she really want to fraternise with this fluorescent shade? You are from the social services, Mevrouw? What? Come closer, chincherinchee, I'm hard of hearing. You're from the service that does the annual census of rough sleepers? She looks at me! Oh, what an expert gaze rests upon me. Diva of the indolents in the catacombs of Krijtberg, sleep-counter of the stone-broke in the Heiligeweg! Or maybe the favourite assistant of Dominee Visser of Rotterdam, and his nomad flock of the Pauluskerk? He'll have a hard time without his scraggy sheep, so needful of his consoling hand. The poor stutterer, turfed out of his congregation by a mob of bureau rats, with matching mutiny in the beggar flock, believe it or not, now we wait for the opera in three acts with a choir of vagrants. The Good Man of Rotterdam. As though one gesticulating killjoy with a gaping hole in his carcass isn't enough there on the foreshore. Citizens, behold how the swallows of the lord fly through my gut!

Memo 4

The reference to Zadkine's statue is for my sake, I think. Posturing to impress me, I write on my clipboard, plus a list of questions. Histrionic personality disorder? Manic depression?

Drunkenness? None of these would be unusual for a vagrant. But this man does not seem disturbed. Angry, yes, maybe with a few drinks under his belt, a fruitcake, a confidence trickster. That's my analysis. But this evaporates under his gaze, a charming, laughing look that contradicts his sardonic tone. Who is this man? I lower my eyes, fiddle with the controls of my tape recorder.

My late brother Willem, the writer, always said that I was a voyeur just like him, but that I chose to present it as disaster relief management with a scientific basis. "Rather dubious, my learned sister, the way you give these helpless people a voice while actually feeding off their confessions. Just as long as you don't get rich doing so."

This was why he'd rather be a poet than a novelist, Willem always said: It would limit him to introspection rather than preying on others.

After my father's death, I started visiting Willem more regularly. It was the first time we'd truly spoken since leaving our childhood home; he was so much older than me, and maybe even more of a rara avis. Now, death has finally liberated him from his characters, he's free from the struggle to camouflage his insatiable ego, just as he always desired; six feet under the sod of Zorgvlied, nothing but innocent bones at last.

But who will write the stories now? I'm no writer. Like you, I am a vagrancy expert, but is there ever science without interest, Professor Sprinkhuizen? And what is the loss of loved ones but a lingering interest in the heart of the one left behind? You can build kingdoms on that, terraria of remembrance. Is this why I write down everything that crosses my mind as I sit there under the elm with the radiant vagrant?

In the mornings, my father would put his address, which I'd typed on a small piece of paper, into his shirt pocket and disappear down the street, returning late in the afternoon, delivered by the florist on a carrier bike. The florist, the fishmonger, the caterer. With a sunflower, a herring, a warm loaf of bread they'd given him, and that he'd present to me with both hands. Then he'd tell me about his adventures, all the strangers he'd spoken to. Sometimes he'd tell me about weird characters following him. In the end, I had him admitted to a care facility. He kept running away, until finally they started locking him in a ward full of dazed people in the mornings, and in the afternoons in a dingy room with burglar bars on the window.

With my questionnaire and my microphone, next to my interlocutor, these memories flutter through me like dandelion seeds; they are drawn into his slipstream, a ship sailing alongside me. I feel the salt spray on my face. I wipe my mouth with the back of my hand before I ask the next question.

Transcription: Recording Snow Sleeper, tape index 6

Where I'm from, that's what you want to know, Mevrouw? Don't they teach the art of the diplomatic approach any more, there in your lieweherehogereschool? "Where" a vagrant is "from", did you hear that, dear listeners? Where from!

Fromness is for someone with a bed in one place, dear lady, but I sleep outside, I come from a cucumber and I blow where I will, I know all the spots, the summer houses and the short stays, this park bench is my Xanadu, but I'm actually a man of snow, I drink my own thirst, with a horseradish for a nose and three chestnut buttons on my stomach, a cruel infestation of imaginings in my breast.

Memo 5

In the afternoon, when I came to visit, Father would be sleeping in front of the snowing television in his room, snow inside, snow outside, his last December, and at five o'clock a nurse would come and walk him down to the courtyard. Is the world still out there? he'd ask. There's nowhere to get lost in here. On his last afternoon, he picked a sprig of holly and put it in the buttonhole of the nurse's uniform, she told me, shook her hand and said "Prettige Kerst" and thank you for the walk, and that he was ready for the canal lock now. She thought it was part of his gobbledygook.

Transcription: Recording Snow Sleeper, tape index 7-9

Mevrouw, let me put it this way: From my palanquin I've been watching my following over the years, they who watch me through a loupe as though I'm a barbarian with my dangler in a gourd. For eighteen years I've been a hobo, and, in the eyes of my fellow man, nothing but a topic, something picturesque, somebody to convert, a field of research, rustling refuse that you'd prod with the tip of your shoe, but nobody's ever asked me, hey, how did you get this fucked?

Shouldn't you be more interested in that?

But where I come from, that's what you want to know! The glow-worm in the sooty kitchen! Where I'm from, Mevrouw, is my mother's lap. And that's where I'm going, too. And you, Mevrouw? Or were you immaculately conceived?

Oh, don't look so aghast, I'm merely the MC for these global calamities.

Come, put your hand on your mount of Venus and observe the evening, like a dove she descends upon the nest of the world, like a poppy she lowers her head to the horizon. My turtledove who ties up my days in her little black scarf, my poppy who dries my words in her skull like fine black sand. I am homeless, I steer by the Dog Star, I eat barley gruel. Do you have a euro for me? Shall I put my eel in your purse to try and sire a smile? Look, Mevrouw, look at the people strolling closer once again, you ensure an audience for me here in the dusky silence, pirates at the last golden buoy beyond the breakwater.

Memo 6

I ignore his innuendoes. My attitude, as prescribed, is empathetic but distant, with reflection of feeling, and alert to incidental information, in order to ascertain the coherence and mental status of the subject. The more I listen to his "obdachloser Unsinn", as he calls it, the more I realise that he's well aware of policies concerning the homeless, he knows about the plan for free accommodation in shipping containers, and the process of removing the marginalised from the inner city. In Amsterdam, if a rough sleeper is found frozen in an alley, he tells me, "they bury him upright in an ecofriendly cardboard box with a nickel tag on his toe". This would've been a flea market of material for Willem, I write on my clipboard.

That's what his house looked like in the end anyway, a flea market. I wouldn't have known what to do with it. Now old Kippelstein is brooding over it, the friend he appointed as his literary executor. Sometimes he phones me to come and lend a hand. But it's always the same story, "The Clockmaker", that he wants me to read to him. He thinks it's about him, but he's too scared to read it himself. Willem's stories are only about Willem, I want to say to him, but the old guy looks so forlorn, why would I rob him of his illusions?

Transcription: Recording Snow Sleeper, tape index 10

Yes, Mevrouw, I am "in possession of an identity document", what a terrible word, why do you have to write up your investigation in this tepid goose-shit type of language? I'm "in possession of" an "identity number", yes, sure, I'm on record with the municipality as a vagrant, as an "avoidant delinquent", because nobody in this country is allowed to move from bed to pisspot without a name, a number, a category. You may weigh me as much as you like, in my balls there's an ounce of spunk you may take to measure my fecundity, and with your callipers you can measure from my nose spout to my earlobe to determine the extent of my hybrid vigour. My postbox? At De Veste in the passage, Querido's night shelter. And no, I don't carry my papers with me, where I'm from the pickpockets would steal the bread from your mouth, so I keep it in my safe, my papers and my gold and my loving kindness.

My full names? My surname? Christened? Oh, don't make me laugh, within me the names romp like the Gadarene swine. Arturo Rosenblut, Gaspard de la Nuit, Lothario Senzatetto, Cardinal Stefaneschi, Woyzek if you please, or Casimir von Slippenbach, I'm similar to my dissimilarity on every point, the dogman of Sinope, my sword is in my pants, two blue berries hang from the hilt, would you like to see them? You say no thank you? Then I shall lift my cap. Under it, there are also two lobes, bomzis and bomzas with an antenna through my fontanelle for reception without interference from hell. Actually I'd like to tell you how I fucked out last year in the shiverling.

Memo 7

At times he speaks Rotwelsch or Bargoens, or some or other rural or colonial dialect, sometimes formal Dutch, all peppered with obscure references, and like clockwork the promise of a "snow story", a "winter's tale" he wants to tell, but first a psalm to "lubricate" me, one of many that he dreams up throughout the interview. He is "cherry-picking from his skullpan" for me, he says. Obviously hoping for a contribution in his shoe, "por Dios".

Somehow the tune of the psalm is familiar. Is it the same one the janitor at the home was humming in the storeroom when I fetched my father's suitcase? He walked ahead of me down the narrow passages, his keys jingling on his belt, there were shelves to the ceiling, bags and suitcases in every size and colour. Before, we were able to keep the deceased's things here for a few years, Mevrouw, he said, some next of kin need a bit of time before they come to fetch them. Some never come. Now we donate it to a charity organisation after three months. But we have a backlog, as you can see. He had a list of my father's last belongings that I had to check against the contents of the suitcase. I opened the latches, then closed them. Never mind, I said, it doesn't matter any more.

Transcription: Recording Snow Sleeper, tape index 11

We travel as though captive
Still through a foreign land
Wretched outcasts of the world
Unseen and never heard
But when they do regard us
Then they shall hear us sing
Of wondrous benefaction
Our journey's end shall bring.

Memo 8

The psalm is sung in a stentorious tremolo. He sings with his head tilted upwards, as if addressing a high pulpit, a vulnerable old tune that resounds among the late blackbird sounds. Silence descends as he finishes. Without touching me, his hand brushes down my back. One day, he promises, somebody will page open my "frêle scapulas" in order to stitch angel wings to them, and then at least there will be some marrow of truth in my backbone. Nobody wants to believe what happened to him, he says, looking me right in the eye, and surely the reason I'm beside him here on the bench is because I want to believe in something?

I think: I can end the interview, put away my tape recorder and just have a conversation with him. A meeting on a park bench, surely this happens sometimes? The questions I would ask aren't on my list. Who was the vagrant's mother, for example. That he had to get away from her? Had to look for her his entire life? I try to complete my Communication Wheel Diagram: vocabulary, articulation, coherence, connection. He gets the maximum points, the wheel wasn't designed for this, he presses his finger on the solid pink circle, makes a sound like a wolf trap slamming shut.

Transcription: Recording Snow Sleeper, tape index 12

Come, come, Mevrouw, forget about your diagram now, even the roses are yearning, their pink is more dependable than your felt-tip pen. I'll carefully package my snow story for you. It's all in the packaging, isn't it? The prologue, the first sentence, the delay before the ending, and bang, the shackle around your ankle. I know, it's how I earn a living, with thrilling stories, maybe you'll give me something in return, a sniff in your nape, a clue to your tabernacle?

She smiles? She finds this entertaining? A queen led up the garden path by a clown with a donkey cock in his pantaloon?

Look, she's preparing to document me, my documentress, she crosses her legs, she wants to indemnify herself against the dildo of my deepest thoughts.

Memo 9

I try to suppress a smile. As though this is the sign he's been waiting for, he puts out his hand for me to shake. A soft hand, a warm hand for a hobo. He calls me a "ragged magpie on his scrapheap", promises that his saga will be a whole chapter of my dissertation (when did I tell him about that? Or is this just part of his swindling?), and also "commentaries and glossaria and many years' chirruping in my daycare or asylum or the tower of my socially responsible investigation" or whatever the fuck I call my "homeless lobby". Fuck the housing, heaven is my shepherd, he cries with his arms open wide. "Not to autumn will I yield, not to winter even." Where would he have got that from?

We agree: I have my questionnaire and he has his story, I want the general and he wants the specific, I want numbers and he wants clarity. So can we call it quits, he asks: I ask a question and get a usable answer, and then he tells a part of his story. Between your inquisition and my serial, he says, we can take turns breaking wind and making stars. And then we have a concert on the park bench for Madonna, homeless man and evening hens, and for him this is enough, not many people can converse with him on his level, he says. (According to the encyclopaedia, this is a reference to the Pleiades, to Freya's hens, not the first time he's referred to Scandinavia, maybe he's been there on his travels?) I look at his profile, sorrowful mouth, determined chin. Is this the kind of stranger my father would have met on his travels through the city? The kind that he would come and tell me about in my study, as if to say, get out there and get to know yourself, life experience can't be gained by reading books.

Only after his death could I start that task, go out into the city alone on a Friday night, learn to play with whatever crosses my path.

Transcription: Recording Snow Sleeper, tape index 13

You ask what problems I, as a homeless person, experience daily?

Finding a place to defecate, Mevrouw, is a pain for a tramp. Deodatus, my compatriot from Schiermonnikoog, he prefers the Public Library, he says the hallowed halls of the book really get his bowels going. I prefer the train from Amsterdam to Sloterdijk. I prefer to bum a shit.

From my rough slumber under my rough cardboard I wake, and I shake myself from my rough dreams like a rough dog and proceed to the station. I greet my brothers waving their scaly gazettes. We wish you a good start, a soft stool, Kasparus, they call. We know one other's faces, we know what we look like when we need to take a shit. I fling a quarter into the hat of the gypsy and he plays me a poop tattoo on his trumpet.

A peregrino in my coat, masked by my beard, I'm first to board, and head straight for the smelly little toilet in second class. The window open for background noise, I lift the lid, drop my pants and arrange my buttocks on the seat. And I open myself, aha, even before the whistle blows.

Listen to my fantasy, Mevrouw: My gut is in a gut and my bolus is in a bolus. You see, every morning the train gobbles up its passengers, buttered up with expectation, and shits them out through the sluices onto grey platforms, the fat egos of our fatherland in their gutters brimming with wisdom. The yellow train on its straight tracks is their fixed passage, as it used to be mine.

Yes, yes, I'm a well-read man, Mevrouw, as you can surely hear. I am a student of the dogs. Inside the busy channel I sit, homunculus karpunculus, turning my tiny unpaid-for hobo turd composed of the scraps from chip stalls. From Amsterdam to Sloterdijk lies the shit chute of Kasparus the potato fox. My fallout can be scraped up and marketed as guano, to be applied to strawberries. Yes, why not on the front page of de Volkskrant, *I, minister sans parliament, with the greenest eco-footprint?*

Oh, the peristalsis of the train, Mevrouw, the doors floop shut with a hiss, and that first pulse, the grinding in the daylight of steel on steel, and there I sit with the infernal racket all around and I relax my sphincter, staring at the tips of my boots, considering my existence. My shitting stool is my prayer stool, that is correct, Madame, the seat of morning prayers, there I mutter my priceless prayer in the incense rising from my arse, and sing my prelude to the day, utterly god-ridden with delight.

And what you know is what you do not know.
And what you own is what you do not own.
And where you are is not where you are.

Memo 10

When I was small, my father built me a swing in the back yard, with red and yellow poles and chains and a smooth plank for a seat. He thought I lacked breath, movement, merriment. Because I didn't have a mother, he was anxious about raising me properly. Play among the clouds, my girl, learn about them. A few years after I fetched him to come live with me in the city, he asked me one morning at breakfast if I could remember the colours of the swing's poles. I asked if he remembered what he always said to me about the clouds, and what he meant by it. I noticed that his eyes were moist, his mouth hesitant, that he stirred five teaspoons of sugar into his tea, tried to hang the newspaper on the hook for the dishcloth behind the door. I thought it was one of his Zen jokes. Until he stood in front of me at bedtime the next evening with his pyjamas folded in his hands, and asked me what he was supposed to do with this. I helped him to put them on. You're with the clouds again, Dad, I whispered as I drew the covers up to his chin, and he said, rather there than at rock bottom, child.

In the months before he went to the home, we often sat with him in the tiny garden behind the house with our grey heads, his whiter than mine and Willem's, and identified the clouds as we'd done when we were small: seagull, teapot, peony, galleon. He always saw more outlandish things than we did, and knew stranger words: broccoli romanesco, guilloche, piebald.

Could the hobo sense I had other things on my mind? This man with the tongue of a bandit?

Sometimes he'd ask to hear his comments played back, he wished to improve his "rhetoric"; take two, take three, take four, until I objected because I only had three tapes.

Transcription: Recording Snow Sleeper, tape index 14

Satisfied? Can you use my answers? And now it's my turn, Mevrouw. Let me first give you some background on my clients. For the scientist I am a research area, for city sanitisers a statistic. I sit for painters, I stand up straight for mimes, flutter like elm seeds under brooms, I stuff myself into lampposts for sniffer dogs, I hoist my balls to escape the pet stoats of gangster boys, I let my light shine for the lord, I support the jenever distiller on the Overtoom, I am an ornament with exhaust fumes, a pissing-pole for poodles, an employer of railway cleaners, a source of endless nonsense, like the wallpaper of dreams. Like a ribbon from the mouth of the angels, I excrete the mirages of my past. I am the cloak of the mist, the sob in the neck of a swan, the child in the lathe of parental misunderstanding. But I don't subject myself, I improvise my face, I am king of the brume, concert master of the snow. The winter often blesses me with unexpected glories. In the summer I tell it all in other people's stories.

Memo 11

From the corner of my eye, I see him looking at me inquisitively. I remain laconic, knowing that by withholding my curiosity, I'm encouraging the narrator. He plays along, stays quiet for some time, takes a pear from his plastic bag and a knife from his pocket and starts peeling the fruit, carefully dropping a thin spiral in his lap. A pear made of light and air, you see? he says, and lifts the peel slightly with the tip of the knife before letting it curl up again. He slices off one of the pear's cheeks and offers it to me, but I decline politely, just as the rulebook says. If I were to eat a pear with you, I think, I might just tell you everything about the orchards of my youth.

Transcription: Recording Snow Sleeper, tape index 15

For example, Mevrouw, two winters ago I was quite the find for a student from the Third World. He wore a waistcoat and a butterfly tie, he had feverish eyes, he was lost in the city, stood with his forehead against the glass of shops, and in a small black notebook wrote things about cobblestones in the streets. He longed for revelation, peering into the water where the dredgers hauled up waste from deep below. Tables, chairs, bicycles, skeletons, walking frames, everything hanging there in the cactus claw, dripping. He recorded everything, as if they were the treasures of Atlantis. And then, as though sent by Orpheus, a swan swims through the slime sucked up from the bottom, and what does the boy do? He glows as though he's just seen his god. I followed him to his home on the Geldersekade and I watched him. A voyeur of nothing! No, not me, Mevrouw, him! For hours on end he'd stand at his window with opera glasses watching the Liebherr cranes, the façade of the library, the reflections of the gables, and every time a swan came by he'd blow on the window and write lorem ipsum in the vapour. Then he'd erase it with his sleeve and stand with his forehead against the window frame, like a stained-glass angel with a bow tie.

I want to tell you about this type, Mevrouw. They are almighty alms-givers, these placeholders of nothing, they are quite willing to sell their own souls for some insight into their own disorientation. And this is what I make possible for them. They are the people who offer me a day's worth of honest work. And I, the faceless one, play the mirror for their fantasies and self-abnegation. Yes, you're laughing, I've been exploited by masochists my whole life. A wretched person like me, recorded, photographed, registered, captured, should get commission for my contribution to the Rijksprentenkabinet and other halls of artistic treasures. But I don't even get a lean-to! What can I do in the end but avenge myself? On behalf of all the wretches who've sat as models through the ages so that narcissists on state subsidy can excrete artworks?

And how do I do this, exactly?

I find a place to sleep in a portico, right across the street from this student with the binoculars, and yes, I appear to him, Mevrouw. I stay in the shadows, and calculate the moment, and step into the floodlights of his awareness. I gesticulate. I mumble to the heavens. I speak to the swans. I become a magician, just as he wishes. In two minutes he's at the bottom of the stairs, ready to meander into the depths. And I lead him all over the city on routes to nowhere, I cast bread on the water, he thinks I'm a wizard, can you believe it. Three days later he tugs at my sleeve and invites me to share his home, and I know that as long as I keep quiet, I'm as safe as a shah. I feed his hunger for fairy tales and he serves me from his grandiose heart. Pumpkin soup and roast chicken he prepared before me, scrubbed my scabby spots and clothed me all in white as if I were a prince from Mauritania. But make no mistake, Mevrouw, there comes a point where one tires of playing the king to such a slave, and after three months I left him, the snuffhead. He disappeared for a few months, but he's back now, I see him sometimes; he has become one of us, talks to the swans, stays around the Oosterdok between the construction-site huts, but he doesn't recognise me without my rope ladder and my old coat that's losing its down stuffing.

I've had a new disguise for some time now. I wear glasses without lenses and pretend to be a has-been actor. Now don't look at me like that, Mevrouw, you too have an abyss in your back yard.

Memo 12

Is this a warning, this tall tale about the fate of the student? Is that what he's getting at? Trying to teach me a lesson?

Bamboozlers, that's what my father called his type, but he also read me and Willem thumb-sucked stories from the newspaper when we were small, pretending to follow the lines with his eyes. That's where Willem got his ideas. There's no fun in just a story, he always said, what matters is the sliding frame of the presentation, and all the hidden asides. Actions and events must be repeated, reversed or miniaturised, slowed down or sped up, within the framing of the story. The author must be portrayed in the narrator of the story, who in turn tells a story about someone telling a story, and so on. Or vice versa. The design of the framework is the tricky part. Who tells what to whom, when, where, why and especially how, that's the point, therefore a novel is always at least two novels, preferably a story within a story within a story, the activation of an infinite regression, with the end swallowed whole by the beginning. No one must think for a minute that they're on solid ground, it must work like the Klein bottle in mathematics.

All my life I've been half fascinated, half infuriated by these affectations. A straight-laced child, an organiser, serious and caring, and especially wary of clowns, I had to be seduced to take part in frivolousness.

But what's this, tugging at my sleeve on this summer's evening?

On my stomach with my cheek to the ground, my father taught me how to knock back at dung beetles with a small stone on the hard-baked clay, carefully in the same rhythm, with the right silences in between, until it came into view, the shiny black tapping beetle, marching on its hook legs against the horizon of grass.

Transcription: Recording Snow Sleeper, tape index 16
Defecation ticked off, Mevrouw? Right then, your second question, typical problems of a homeless person: You asked me where I sleep at

night? O soothest sleep, o soft embalmer of the still midnight! I've also tried to fathom it. Because I am the sidekick of our dear lord in the attic, that old fucker so bored with his faultless creations. The entire seventh day he slept, to figure out how he, the very first sleeper in the universe, could further entertain himself, and from his cellar of omniscience he then concocted the Fall of Man just to keep himself occupied, and voilà, the world is full of baroque evil, thunder and lightning, wars and crucifixions that he drags this way and that while his wingéd castrati sing about the unwithering roses of Jerusalem.

Why I sleep for so many hours, Mevrouw, you want to know that? We are glow-worms of nobody's intention, therefore we must sleep and sleep, under the black poppy of the night. There was a time when I wanted to pick it, the night on a hairy stalk in a glass of water, the calyx a spinning nebula that I wanted to analyse, sweet white whey of wonderment that I wanted to drink when I still used to advocate the importance of words.

Now I drink jenever, at least it gives you a real hangover.

I am a rough sleeper, yes, I find a corner, I find some stairs, I find a bag, I look for a black place to find some thick black sleep, or an alley to blow away in whitely. That I ever thought there were signs and meaning . . . but there is nothing more than sighs, cries, palpitations, the beats of a waltz, the flickering of a candle, a dance of shadow puppets under bridges, over which the more solid ones march at a steady pace to their destinations. Blinded by determination, most of my fellow humans. But you ended up with me; were you really looking for respite here, with a safe-cracker that you think you can audit?

Oh, touch my shoulder, Mevrouw, so that I can feel alive. You, with the two naïve blue eyes. Oh, if only I could dote on women, but now I'm the gatekeeper of my own eternal departure.

You're writing this down? You find it beautiful? No, if I were the mayor, you ask, what would I do about the homeless person's need for sleep? Well, that elegant decoy duck with his chain in the town hall, he could utilise us as living city monuments, viewable for a fee, like Fabiola in the eighties, and then spend that money on free manicures for drifters.

What would I suggest regarding accommodation for the homeless? Well, imagine, Mevrouw, a kind of human croquette wall in the Centraal Station, with sleeping lockers where runaways can insert a coin for some rest, an incubator for clochards, with peepholes for the tourist, a peepshow without equal, my head a fish tin where black sardines swim to the beat of Mozart minuets. Much rather that than De Haven, where you become a schoolboy with blue pyjamas at night and play games of badminton under supervision, under neon lights in the recreation hall, between plastic ficuses. Freshly scrubbed Wotans with shampoo beards and rackets, oars to row them on their long-lost Viking journeys. Chicken soup sloshing in their hairy hobo paunches. Sleep? Well, when I'm tired, I sleep, Mevrouw, write that down, in the rain, in the sunshine, in the snow. I want to tell you about snow, about what happened to me in the Witte Hartensteeg.

Memo 13, 13 July 2008
Today I went outside for the first time since the encounter, fully disguised as a bag lady, complete with wig and rags. An

unnoticed seeker. How many times now have I listened to the recordings? The humming pauses where my voice disappears are bothersome, I would've liked to hear myself talking to him again. Did I really want to hear his story, that night? I couldn't be bothered. Then, as now, it was about finding the lost purse in MacNeice's poem. Who wouldn't, as he writes, want to find the lost coins, Professor? His eyes burning into mine, his language branded onto me, forgotten things emerging from the fog. Was my life not also a kind of Witte Hartensteeg? The endless books, the endless studies, to keep time off my back, to give my life meaning.

Klopje, Willem sometimes called me, and I always thought he was referring to the tapping beetles of our childhood, until Kippelstein told me at his funeral that it was the name of a type of beguine that lived outside a monastery.

But on this park bench, the time flew. In the tree above, swarms of parakeets swished around before settling down for the night, a blood-red sunset, something fruity in the air. A roller skater with lights on his heels whizzed past, a rhythm took hold of our repetitions, inversions, accelerations and delays, as though we were exchanging music, with the memories of my father as a pedal point. My father who, in the end, ate grass in an asylum park, with a napkin around his neck, grass and a dessert of semolina. Where are my glasses, where's my hat, he repeated hundreds of times, he wanted to cycle down the gravel road to Koringberg. They had to prop him up under the shower, his girls in green, he couldn't understand why I was single throughout my life. The ragged soul there in his cage, my old dad who asked me to take his hands and show him how, he'd forgotten how to do it, how to make a rabbit of shadows like he made for me in the light of a candle when I was small . . . And when he'd had enough of that, he looked at me and pointed at the burglar bars, searched for the word, didn't find it, and said: epithalamium.

It's quite something to make a word have meaning, I said. Something flickered in his eyes before he answered: If I make a word work this hard, I always pay it a little extra.

The bag lady's children's book. *Alice in Wonderland*, where had I hidden it all these years? "Alicia in terra mirabilis" – my dad helped me translate little bits into Latin when I was thirteen.

Transcription: Recording Snow Sleeper, tape index 17

You still have so many questions? About my income, my friends, my shoes, my shirt and trousers, you crack the whip in the sawdust circle, it's the circus of the new moon, oh summer's evening where we weave our tapestries, the researcher and her counsellor, by a lantern of longing.

Listen! I was completely fucked, Mevrouw, last winter, I'd had enough, slept in the Witte Hartensteeg, packing myself in newspaper, crates, straw and planks, my own Bethlehem, my own wise man. Each day I'd go to donate plasma to earn a few cents, and then bury myself with my thick salty blood in a cocoon in the snow; at four in the afternoon I'd plunge into the maze of the night with my knapsack of

bread and milk, wade under canals and converse with my predeces-
sors, ghosts of the golden age, with pepper sniffers, with that pickpocket
dissected by Doctor Tulp, and with the treaders of the water wheels,
martyrs of Holland's riches, while the ships full of cinnamon blew
their horns in the docks. In my hut I kept a diary written in cold
ballpoint ink by the light of a small torch. I slept silently there in my
tent of plastic and cardboard, from which I woke unwillingly in the
mornings, a springhare raising its ears before the surprised eyes of the
poacher, emerging from the snow and wiping a half-frozen paw over
its nose.

And yes, I can see the question in your face, who was following
me this time? He thought I didn't see him above me in the alley, a
man pretending to feed sparrows at his window on the third floor,
but I could feel his stare in the small of my back and I could hear his
camera firing away, a photographer I thought, I could see him saying
my name, little clouds of vapour from his mouth: "The Snow Sleeper".
A title I was, all of a sudden! Caption for a picture-maker! The loot of
a light thief! He was the last straw, Mevrouw, the last robber that I
would endure. Pest controllers, psychiatrists, preachers, policemen, I've
had all of them on my case and here was another one, believe it or not,
trying to cheat me out of death, the spoiler of a determined Lazarus. I
was on my way to oblivion and he, the idiot with his photo lenses, was
trying to extend my parole in the land of pancake guzzlers.

And you know what I did then, Mevrouw? I went to stand around
the corner and I watched him, *the fool who was trying to take away*
my ending to make it his own, make it a photostrip. See what he

did to my building materials, folded neatly on my carrier bike every morning, Mevrouw. He unpacked each and every shred of it there in the snow, unfolded every single thing. As though they were Persian carpets, woven cloths of a tent palace. He took out a measuring tape and wrote everything down in the greatest detail, my planks, the crates at my head and feet, my canvas and my plastic, my pieces of foam and jute, my newspapers and my rags, my cables and my ropes, an inventory of every last piece of junk. He dug out my diary and read it and captured every single page on film. Click, click, click for his microfiche, that lowlife. And then he put everything back just like he found it, carefully, Theodorus Popsnor, as though a drifter would be too dim to see the flyshit on his bread.

Memo 14

A fable meant just for me? He strokes my recorder like it's a cat. What makes a tape recorder different to a camera? He interrupts his story with well-considered pauses, hand over hand he draws me in.

Through a glass darkly, face to face, through the valley of the shadow of death, to the quiet waters. That's what my father always whispered to the cows when he helped them to calve, and I sat on the barn wall, the smell of blood and miracles in my nose, that murmuring of his as he knelt there, unrelated fragments bound together by sound, a babbling, uninterrupted, his sleeve rolled all the way up, everything that crossed his mind, his entire childhood, his father's flour mill, his father's overalls, the white dust he helped to beat from them at night, his mother's generosity, one long musical offering of remembrance there beside the cow, brushing her flank, whispering beside the origin of the world, come, little buttermilk, come, little bluegum bloom.

Eli, Eli, lama sabachthani.

Transcription: Recording Snow Sleeper, tape index 18

Your next question, Mevrouw? Maybe I'm boring you with my story? You look at my trousers, my shirt, you ask where I get my clothes? Sometimes from the Volksverbond shop in the Scheepvaartbuurt. Sometimes from a laundry where the clean and anonymous clothes slink in plastic packaging like drained mummies; after three months they give them to the less fortunate, then I walk around in trousers from De Pijp and a shirt from Oud-Zuid and I can see the forgetful recognising their clothes on my back. I'm the walking coatrack of the city, Mevrouw, I pass my days in the shed skins of Ouroboros Amsterdam.

You read my snow-white windbreaker? Golden Tulip, isn't that great? My work livery: I've been advertising for years, unleaded petrol, yacht cruises on the Côte d'Azur, cakes, bacon, cocoa powder from Droste. In Los Angeles the hobos advertise Weigh-Less for Jesus. No better camouflage for a man like me, under my advertisement coat I spin my mirror for the larks, a toy that would enchant you, Mevrouw, have you ever heard of it?

Memo 15

A woman who needs toys? A woman who misses enchantment, who needs re-enchantment? Lately, I've been dreaming about my father's harmonica. They took it away from him in the home. When he woke up at night he'd play on it, that's what the matron told me, "An der schönen blauen Donau", and "Blijf bij mij, Heer", and "En ik ben met Catootje naar de botermarkt geweest". They also took his pocketknife that he used to mark his doorframe every morning, to count the days until I visited again.

The red Swiss Army knife, the silver harmonica, a small pair of pliers that once belonged to his father and that he'd wanted to take along when I went with him to the facility, in the end these were all packed in a suitcase with his clothes. I had to sign below a list. Hat, scarf, dressing gown, seven white handkerchiefs. I put the suitcase in the storage bay under the stairs when I got home. When I go upstairs at night, I cross a high bridge over a river full of cloud reflections. I grip the bannister, I keep my eyes on the crossing and I never look down.

These days, when I can't sleep, I search the recordings for clues. The recorder sits next to my bed, I can press the play button with my eyes closed. I pick things up in the singsong way he pronounces certain words, *lé-werik*, for example. A long, sinking tone and then three stops of lips and tongue and soft palate. Two larks, he once called us, rising in the deep afterglow, dreamy in the last of the light.

"Lewerkie", my father pronounced it when he saw one in a

field. He'd imitate the upward flight with his hands, yodelling, with me clinging to the leg of his trousers, my head barely higher than the sweeping ears of wheat, eyes screwed up against the bright sun to follow the drop, the effortless warbling.

Transcription: Recording Snow Sleeper, tape index 19

Like the last centaur on earth, I picked my spot, Mevrouw, the Witte Hartensteeg, behind P.C. Hooftstraat, uninhabited, mostly unused, I drew my limbs close, rolled myself into a tight ball, picked the dark days before Christmas so that I wouldn't start smelling before I was found, the narrow gate, the dark valley, no fuss, no tam-tam, just my own heart and breath, my own trapdoor to the underworld, throttled in the pack ice with my flashlight, the hum of the city growing ever softer, tenant of my own rustling nest. But then all at once someone wanted to make an artwork of me. Wanted to arrange me better than I'd arranged myself, a model with a vanishing point for someone else's eye, another artist lacking the courage to go and cannibalise himself in his own inner room, but using another person's misery for his experiments in self-discovery.

You think I'm lying, Mevrouw; do you really want to hear the epilogue, or shall I sing another song for your machine, there under the bridge where it echoes so nicely? "Jesus' Blood Never Failed Me Yet"?

Memo 16

Sometimes he rocks gently forwards and backwards in time with his sentences, like a shaman at a birth, as if he wants to help the new arrival find passage into the world. Is it me he's pushing out ahead of him in the mouth of the shaft, behind whom he battens down the hatches? I hold on tight to my questionnaire, like someone clutching at grass and branches as she falls.

Sometimes in the home I sat for hours with my father, behind him on his bed, rocking him like a big grey-haired child, my head against his back, trying to blow some courage into him, the golden images of his fatherhood, the bunch of yellow and blue lupins he brought from the fields, stamping his feet as he arrived home.

Transcription: Recording Snow Sleeper, tape index 20

Have I been in jail? Arrested for a crime? True to my species I am, Mevrouw, an incorrigible sinner. Violator of prohibitions against sleeping, begging, walking on dikes, sauntering aimlessly down a public road, you name it; sometimes I write "no humans allowed" on my stomach and everybody looks the other way. Sometimes I fake an epileptic fit in Dikker en Thijs. Wonderful, that chic lot with hands full of salmon and artichokes, and there I throw a grand mal with a mouthful of bubble bath, bubbles all over the floor. They dump the gravadlax and quiche with French truffles and rush home to eat biscuits covered in chocolate and be embarrassed about their riches while I lick the slop off the floor. But the deed with which I was going to end my laborious cabaret, my gateway to the nether world, I was never prosecuted for that.

The photographer thought he was the one framing me, but I was the one shoving my deceit up his arse like a stick, through his neck and into his skull, turning him into my marionette.

This is the real meaning of a "capital crime", Mevrouw, but it isn't written into law. At exactly four o'clock in the afternoon I appeared in the alley, where he was waiting for me at his window. Here comes my subject, he thought, but he was mine all along! Do you want to know what I did? It was like a straight line of cocaine, mind you. A tip for posterity. Don't fuck with hobos, they'll make you sniff them!

Memo 17

He sat too close to me and spoke very softly, acting everything out with his hands, as if directing me. In the park lamplight, his eyes glowed. We were alone in the rose garden. A breeze in the elm. How had I been sucked into someone else's imagination in just a few hours? Broken open and now at his mercy? I was at the threshold to a parallel world. I switched on the reading light on my clipboard to steel myself, but he took it from me without a word and turned it back off. I was aware of bicycles, the far-off laughter of picnickers, day visitors who didn't want to go home yet, here and there a child's floating paper lantern, flickering cigarette lighters. And I was back, back in those fields where my father wore a headlamp to look for abandoned twin lambs on Easter weekend, carrying them to the farmyard under the stars, a cyclops with the snow-white bleating lambs in his arms, their little hooves dangling against his blue overalls.

Transcription: Recording Snow Sleeper, tape index 21

Listen, I always entered the alley deliberately, Mevrouw, to the beat of a requiem, leaving deep footprints in the snow, so that he could take nice photographs. Then I started building my shelter. Used a piece of iron to scrape the snow from my sleeping spot. Click. Laid two long rolls of plastic on either side of the hollow and a piece of canvas between them on the bare ground. Click, click. The four planks on top of the canvas side by side tied together with metal strips at both ends. This was the base of my bed. The pieces of foam on top, my mattress. Click, he swapped his batteries. The jute bags on the foam, like bedspreads. Click. The wooden crates with the open sides facing inwards, the top and bottom ends of the planks shoved into the bottoms of the crates, and a rope fastened between the tops of the crates above the bed, to serve as a spine for the tent. My writing pad and flashlight, the bundle of straw and rags as a pillow, the newspapers, plastic bags in heaps around my mattress, the cardboard splayed open, ready for me to cover myself with it. Click, click, click. I granted him a profile portrait. Click, clack, smiling to the heavens. How many photographs did you count?

And then the moment he was waiting for, my disappearing act, the rabbit down the cylinder of the top hat into oblivion. With a flash of teeth I dove in, head and feet placed in the open ends of the crates, with red gloves I yanked the jute bags over my body covering myself entirely. Then I blindly grabbed the plastic rolls on either side of me, first the left and then the right, sweeping them up over the rope spine where they hung for a moment like unfurled spinnakers before gracefully descending to cover my shelter like a tent, a sloop under sail, my head-end straining against the snow like a prow.

After an hour I heard him close his window, but through the gaps I could see him still taking pictures. And then I wrote in my book by torchlight, not my own thoughts, but his.

What do photographers think, Mevrouw, when they take photographs of us?

I knew he'd come and take a closer look. I heard him coming from Hobbemastraat, inching closer. Saw his camera flash. Did he press his ear against the side? I lay there, completely still. A glowing coal from the hearth of Hephaestus. And after a while he was gone. I could hear him crunching backwards, erasing his tracks as he went. In vain, in vain! Might as well have left a blood trail for a fox!

Memo 18

How could I go home to sleep tonight, I asked myself. I'd want to go to Westerstraat, where Willem's light would still be on, or to the old-age home to throw a small pebble against a window, wake up, Dad, I heard a tall tale from a funny man. But neither of them was there now.

In silence he peeled another pear, offered me the first piece again. I shook my head. He shrugged. When he'd finished it, he took out his flask and held it out to me. A swig?

Eating and drinking with this character would mean the end of a credible report. I unclipped the staff card from the Dienst O&S from my collar. Again, that near touch of his hand on my back, like the snout of some animal, soft as an eel. I put the microphone between us on the bench, on top of the tape recorder.

How did he supplement his grant, I wanted to know. Forcing himself to be patient, he told me how he faked Tourette's in the flower market, a string of expletives, tifuspokketeringkont, with a gerbera behind his ear for the tourists. But these were old man's tricks. In his younger years he was wild, he told me, he would "touch himself" in the middle of the day in front of sultry perfume ads at the tram stop on the Leidseplein, have debates with his fellow bums in front of bystanders about death, about the State, about work, about rest. "We were brave dogs, a happy, sinister horde with the badge of the bees on our chests", the soulmakers of the city, currently being cleaned out along with the whores and everything else that lives in the margins. Imagine, Mevrouw, he said, the unsweetened marital beds of the burghers who now, for want of whores, have to turn their own wives over if they want an affaire.

I asked him how he came to be homeless. He was silent. After some time he drew brackets in the air. Sent off on a Saturday morning with a friendly note and a piece of gevulde koek, he said, and from then on "the winter light was my destiny".

He took out a packet of tobacco and rolled a cigarette, lit it and offered me a draw, which I declined. Was the blushing apple left on the shelf ready for the picking, that's what he asked me. He placed the tape recorder and microphone in his lap and moved closer to me.

Transcription: Recording Snow Sleeper, tape index 22

I dropped little letters for him in the street, Mevrouw, and he snatched them up as though they were Ariadne's threads. My best nonsense, composed for him at night under two feet of snow, about a king who couldn't remember what he'd dreamt, and would ask his slave in the morning. Shall I recite a piece for you?

All night by the sponde of mon maistre
I wait, Francois Lapin, Valet de Chambre,
et Horloger Extraordinaire de son Majesté,
and wind the springs of the standing clock,
tralalee tralalay
move every hour the enamelled hands
on the shallow face of eternity
keep a running log of his movements
in my silver parchment as he turns over in his bed,
and hang my head and shoulders,
snow tents over his breathing
as it comes and goes
zip-a-dee-doo-dah, zip-a-dee-ay.

And at dawn in his night shirt
on the chaise longue of the light
calls the king: my little buck-rabbit wakingslave,
tell me, if you hold your life most dear,
what did I dream, I cannot recall.

And then I divine for him the log
of hours at which his knuckles had clicked,
or he farted and thrashed around in bed
or his magnificent turtledove veered up in his crotch
and from the signs of his body I weave
the most fitting flights of fancy
hickory dickory dock, the mouse ran up the clock
and that sort of thing.

Schon gut, Rote Roermund,
the king then always cries,
Stromkarlen von Unten
you are my purple ragwort
and I belong to you.

And then he puts a sugar cube on my tongue,
in my gob, in the middle of my lick,
in the gutter of all lies.
Tralalee, tralala! Zip-a-dee-doo-dah, zip-a-dee-ay.

How do you like that, Mevrouw? Just one line at a time on a tiny
scrap of paper, folded tightly. And then I watch from behind a tree
trunk as he pieces together the little bits of shit to try and make sense
of the whole. Slip-slop, I let him follow me through the melting ice
over the Museumplein to the Spiegelgracht where I position myself
in front of the antiquarian's window to watch him in the reflections.

A mutual peepshow, with an added clockmaker wondering why I'm staring so intently at the miroir aux alouettes. And I'm constantly being photographed from behind by that rubberneck, click-clack with his camera.

Memo 19

Would that have been the shop of old Kippelstein, Willem's friend?

It wasn't a good time to ask. He leaned away from me and chuckled softly, pulled his fingers through his hair and sang a fragment in English, about Wanderlust, something about the golden pavilions of a garden, about somebody hiding among the blooming trees . . . About calling to her at the garden gate, in passing, and gone is his face.

There was a plum tree in the garden of my youth, a tree that was covered in snow-white blossoms every spring, like a bride, my father always said. In the early summer, when the plums started setting, he was always spraying for codling moths, and in summer when the tree was covered in fruit he rubbed the bloom off on his sleeve to show us the dark purple-red skin. There were also two pear trees, last survivors from an earlier orchard. One winter, a storm blew down all three trees and my father had them cut up for firewood. How those stumps glowed that winter, the plum tree's a deep red with little blue flames, the pear wood, which was slower to burn, with bright yellow hands.

If you're going to split your fire for me, I wanted to tell the drifter, if that's what your story is about, about how you consume people by whom you feel threatened, then I will burn like the wood of a plum tree, you will see all your language burn, soaked into my fibres, you will hear the echo of your impossible tale, a suitcase full of popping coals.

But how could I say something like that?

Transcription: Recording Snow Sleeper, tape index 23

And when you run out of questions, what will you do with me then, Mevrouw? Have me arrested? What can I tell my compatriots at the soup kitchen tomorrow morning? A Scheherazade with a thousand and one questions? Where do you shit where do you sleep what do you eat? They will say, fuck, Grasshopper, can't you dream up something better?

Friends? Of course I have friends, Mevrouw, you want to know how many, not who they are, that's quite clear, so why don't you count them yourself. There's the aforementioned Deodatus, expert on the shithouse in the library, we read the newspapers there together, Mink who catches mice in a bottle and Gwendolyn with the saxophone, and dark Keetman who sometimes gives me a night indoors, and Shmul and Crocodile who show up every now and then from Antwerp, and the Emerald of Jacobsdal with the unflinching paintbrush, Fish the country lady, every day a different burg, Pi the coconut polisher, Berthe, formerly of the convent, who hears me out word for word, and overworked Portegees who provides me with cardboard boxes, and oh and dear, the little Wilhelmina of my heart with the tear hanging from her nipple, yes, runaways make good lovers if only someone sings to them. How often do I see them? Once a day, once a week, the ones I love most once every six months. One must be sparing with one's fondness so that it can last longer. And may I henceforth see you as a friend too, the good truffle of Troy, where do you live, if I may ask? Are you, visitor to the homeless, well housed yourself? Does your office have a refrigerator and a computer? A private telephone?

Because you see, that's one thing I could really use, a free telephone to make a call from every once in a while, when I order a bed in De Veste, for example. You can't take chances, you have to make a booking beforehand. You're not a guest but a client. Even if you've gone to seed, you're still a seedy client. The days are long gone when an extra place was set with straw at the table for the unexpected stranger.

Memo 20

He'd set me a place, and prepared course after course right before my eyes, and I sat stupefied by the spread, clumsy with the cutlery.

Willem always explained that he did his best writing when distracted by something, that too direct a focus on the story would kill it, so he drank and smoked, listened to everything from Bach's Magnificat to *Ummagumma* by Pink Floyd while slyly trying to write the story with the other hand. My father always thought that Willem made mountains out of molehills, he found his stories artificial. Storytelling should be about togetherness and giving joy, it should be like chamber music, he said, a communal creative practice, it should not be the intimidating concert of a virtuoso, but rather a kind of social massage: It doesn't solve any serious problems, but it can rub out a burp or two, and in its rubbing and bearing down, other things might bubble up that have nothing at all to do with the story.

Willem thought my father was old-fashioned.

What would they think of this scene, myself and the vagrant? My brother behind his binoculars, my father behind the snow-covered fir? How would they see me? A strange late bloom. What would they advise me in this situation? Invite him home? Take the suitcase out from under the stairs and give it to him? Seven handkerchiefs and a harmonica?

Transcription: Recording Snow Sleeper, tape index 24

How long did I string the photographer along? A week, Mevrouw, ten days, until I saw he was hooked. I led him all over the city until he was spent, his pockets bulging with my nonsense scraps. I followed him right into the university where he checked some references to try and decipher my poem, as though it was written in some sort of code. Look, I said to Deodatus, there's the man who thinks he can use a needle to tease out a genie curled up in a bottle, but his days are numbered.

Then one day he left an offering at my carrier bike: wine, a baguette and a slab of yellow cheese, while I much rather would've liked a bowl of hot pea soup, but that's what you get from a picture-maker that gets fixated on a clochard, he stuffs him into a box of clichés, including his diet.

He probably wanted me to fall to my knees and thank him for the cheese and pose naked for him. Poor forked animal, I could just about see the caption.

You seem disturbed, Mevrouw, but let me tell you, in the same bag as the baguette, I found from my benefactor batteries for my flashlight, twelve new pencils and a writing pad from the Hema. The equipment of heroes, all I needed was a cloak to make me invisible. Yep, that's how far he went in his neighbourly love. And my notebook? He kept that for himself, Mevrouw, and also my ballpoint. The idiot, he thought he was going to complete my nonsense: in my book, in front of his radiator with cello cantilena and a piece of fish from Albert Heijn.

But then I disappeared.

And I left his bag of brotherly gifts untouched there in the snow.

And I waited around the corner in the Witte Hartensteeg.

Memo 21

Was it just my imagination or had his voice grown somewhat chilly? Was he angry because I wouldn't succumb, even though I had no idea to what, or how? I pulled my legs up higher on the park bench and hugged my knees. Just like I always did on Willem's couch when he read me his latest atrocity, like I did with my dad in his last room in the home, on his bed, while he stared out of the window at the falling snow, all his words forgotten, my brother, my father, their words like clouds, like roses.

I was suddenly hungry, a burning sensation in my stomach.

Den uil die op de peerboom zat.

That's the last thing I sang to Dad. Oy oy oy it's a thatch-roof house.

He looked at me and asked me where I was from, and what my name was.

Transcription: Recording Snow Sleeper, tape index 25

You are the first person I've told my story to, Mevrouw, and you want to know, just before the climax, how many times a week I have a hot meal? Never in my goddamned life have I met someone so rigidly unwilling to say: and then? What happened then? Please go on! Where did you unlearn this skill, Mevrouw, through what attack of constipation?

Anyway, you are the shepherdess of your own salvation, like he was, the arsehole; I could predict what he'd do if I disappeared. He was worse than a junkie going cold turkey. The fool went to my empty spot every morning and stared at it as though he were reading a crystal ball. I watched him from the sewer.

And finally, yes, I was witness to this, just as I expected, he finally built himself a hut there in my very own spot. With my *materials! And buried himself with the bag of food and stationery. With* my *flashlight! In* my *alley! In* my *name! But he couldn't keep himself warm by writing, alas, his story was just too thin, he was a journalist, you see. His medium was camera flash and news, not the loose, warm tongue over the windpipe on which poetry depends. I broke into his apartment on the third floor and stayed there for the night at twenty-five degrees, smashed his cameras in the shower, ripped up his film, pissed in his coffeepot, looked down into the alley at noon, and there he was – under my heap of junk with a stiff arm sticking out in the snow, a sheet of paper clamped in his frozen fist.*

No, Mevrouw, why do you want to leave now? What for? Have you heard enough? I have it here with me, here in my back pocket, his last words, the end of my fairy tale about the king, completed by the dead man, the worst ending you could possibly dream up, not even remotely worth burying yourself alive for. Here, read it yourself. You seem upset? Come now, Helena of the summer's evening, you've sat here the whole time and now you're getting cold feet? Let me turn on your clipboard lamp, as luck would have it you're a wise virgin who charged her batteries.

Memo 22

There was nothing on that sheet of paper, at least, not anything I could decipher, just a fine, regular rippling of pencil marks in lines that curved down at one end like a waterfall. I looked at it and gave it back to him; it was a theatre prop, like the pears, the hip flask, the begging-shoe.

My tape recorder started beeping, an indication that it was almost out of recording time. He told me what was supposedly written on the sheet of paper, the ending the photographer had written for the fable of the king and the chamber slave.

According to him, the king woke from a dream one morning. It was the first time in his life that he could remember what he'd dreamt. He called the slave and told him the dream, in such a boring and long-winded manner that the poor guy who'd been guarding his bed all through the night, every night, almost dozed off on the chaise longue. But he was grateful that at least this time the dream was being recounted by the dreamer himself. From then on, the problem was a thing of the past, and they could get on with their lives, each in his own role. The king put on his crown every morning and ascended his throne and made laws, and the slave plucked the king's nose hairs, made the bed, emptied the commode and wound the clocks, his work finished for the day. In the afternoons he could sit in the shade with the other slaves, singing songs of far-off lovers and lost fatherlands.

Memo 23

It was long after midnight by the time the third tape was full. I thanked the subject for his cooperation, his time, his trouble. There were no longer any people in the park, and I was afraid he might seize the recorder from me and destroy the material, like he had done with the photographer's negatives.

If he'd been exuberant in his welcome, he was melancholic in his farewell, obviously unsatisfied with the outcome. Can you believe it, he asked, that a story finisher would want to help such a bumbling king and his brave slave by cutting them apart, by ironing out their unusual bond, and by turning each of them into a state portrait? Ruler, servant? Peace, order? Living happily ever after?

There was a long silence. I thought about the day I visited

my dad's room in the home for the last time. Somehow, he'd managed to get his hands through the burglar bars and push open the windows. He was in his chair, which he'd drawn up to the window; some snow was blowing in, with the black shape of a fir behind it, a white chunk of snow on every branch. I wiped the ice crystals from his face, found his mouth in a smile, knew it was from managing to open the window: the contentment of knowing he'd seen to it himself that whatever it was, and however it arrived, he could face the wind that carried it, in front of an open window, without obstruction or impediment.

Beside me, the snow sleeper had cleared his throat a few times, started a sentence a few times. Would you, could you, can you, but he didn't get any further. He came and stood in front of me, held his hands beside my face on both sides, not touching. I could feel the heat from his palms on my cheeks, the smell of pears filled my nose, his big dark body obstructed my view, the buckle of his belt gleamed before my eyes. I could feel that he was looking down at me, but I wouldn't look up. He sat down again.

After a while, he started again, this time in a businesslike tone, arguing that it was obviously all quite different in the end, that he'd dug the photographer from the snow at the last minute and used CPR and called an ambulance on the man's cellphone, after which the poor guy was taken away by rescue workers, and that the photographer issued a press statement the day after his release from hospital praising the help, no, the lesson he, a foolish tourist, got from a drifter, and donated a large sum of money to him for his trouble, he still had the clipping in his safe at De Veste, he could show it to me if I cared to walk back there with him.

When it became clear that I would most certainly be leaving on my own terms, he regarded me sternly and started calling me all sorts of names while pretending to sprinkle water on my forehead: "rose without hip fat", "unpainted hoist beam", "blind cinnamon diver", "tremulant apprentice". He would hound me wherever I go, and I mustn't act like I was a "fox terrier in a sputnik". He tailed me for a while, yelling that he would never again take part in any survey of homeless people. That the researchers were poorly trained amateurs who refused to provide debriefing after they, as he put it, had extracted the back teeth of Gargantua in his cave. What this kind of giant needed, he bellowed, with his hand on his chest under the statue of the city virgin at the entrance to the Vondelpark, is a dance partner not a confidentiality agreement, because the latter, he said, meant nothing, that all I wanted in any case were excuses to get rid of him as he was and is and would be, and that what he'd told me was worth less than "resin and pig bristles", but that this was his only consolation, or rather, ammunition in the battle against the bureaucratic enemies of the "charismatic megafauna" that he belonged to, along with the elephant, the panda and the Bengal tiger.

Addendum 19 October 2008
On a whim, I went to the city archives yesterday. It was a lesson in the exclusionary measures these institutions erect against

eccentrics. You see, I was in my bag-lady costume, and was refused entry, but luckily I had my student card and my identification from the Dienst O&S with me. Covert operation, I said, and took off my hat and my wig, after which the friendly archivist proceeded to show me the way.

A cursory look at a random file of photographic material from the past year's exhibitions provided irrefutable evidence, much to my amazement. A group of photos entitled "The Sleeper in the Snow, a Photo Essay" by an anonymous person or persons working under the name of "Brief Moments of Light / Brewwe Ligmomente", exhibited in March of this year. I have been unable to find this organisation on any list of photographic studios. The photos contain tangible evidence of the Schapenburgerpad, as well as abstract photos of the snow-covered heap of packing material, but in the whirl of superimposed light and dark planes I cannot discern a single human figure.

I now realise the problem, Professor: If the subject told the truth, these photographs could not exist. He broke the cameras and destroyed all the film. The only other explanation is that the snow sleeper is not who he says he is, but that he himself is the photographer . . . or was . . .

But who, then, was the victim? If there was, or is one? So I want to check the mortuary registers. Maybe, with a cover letter from your desk, on behalf of the Dienst O&S, I shall be able to access records of unsolved deaths in the city during the relevant period?

Postscript

In the end, I think, this is not where the real riddle lies. Everything up to this point has been preparation, that much is clear. I have even dragged my father's things from under the stairs.

Like every day since the incident, after my discovery in the archives I went back to that park bench in the rose garden, peeled a pear, drank a thimbleful of jenever and blew a mouthful of notes on my father's harmonica.

I am a woman who has been brought into readiness. The end is within me. I am the ending. For me, the apprentice, the suitcase is now open.

The Friend

A Lecture[iii]

Honourable chair, members of the lecture committee,

Until last night, the title of the lecture I was going to deliver here today was: "Mimesis, Poiesis, Parody: The Responsibility of the Imagination and the Boundaries of Photography in Turbulent Times". But early this morning, when I wanted to take this box (*pick up the wooden box and put it upright on the table*) back to the antique dealer Meulendijks en Schuil on Kerkstraat – Amsterdam connoisseurs will know that Mr Schuil has taken over the collection of Kippelstein en Zoon on the Spiegelgracht – I realised that my theme was not the politics of representation, but something much more important. Therefore, I do not wish to indulge in a philosophical speech – nor, certainly, to present a scholarly argument. Rather, I want to tell you about what happened between me and my friend, the photographer Peter Schreuder (*touch the box*). And I want to let you see what is in here before I take it back to a place where it can cause no further harm.

Referencing photography instead of literature today is a further deviation from the usual format, but I have my reasons. Those of you familiar with the South African photography scene would know that Peter Schreuder has been known since the seventies as a photographer of all manner of South African conditions. His last work consisted of portraits of criminals on the Cape Flats in 2007. Some of you may have noticed that he has disappeared from public view, and that no new photographs have been published since.

Well, ladies and gentlemen: My friend Schreuder has been sitting under the fig tree in my back yard for two years now, day in, day out. He has destroyed his cameras. The black cloth he always draped over the tripod is bundled up in a cupboard in my house. He no longer opens his eyes. He cannot, or will not, speak to me. He answers only the birds. I often ask him: Can you ever forgive me? I touch his shoulder and say: I am sorry. It is not clear whether he hears me or not. He is no longer of this world.

I came to know Schreuder at university in the early seventies: a failed economics student who stayed on for several years as an assistant in the Fine Arts department, a helper in the library. Everybody called him "Mister Schreuder", jokingly, because he was quite the opposite of a Mister: no moustache, no religious affiliation, no political party; basically a nobody. The fact that he had not completed his degree was not even his greatest short-coming; that honour befell his exemption from military service due to mild epilepsy. You see, in those days, in certain circles in South Africa, a man who could not say he had been in the army was as good as dead.

Schreuder made a living taking photos at graduation cere-monies. But Stellenbosch, as you would know, was actually a place where girls from the countryside came to find a husband – even today, weddings offer the most lucrative opportunities for a local photographer. But pious brides against backdrops of church steeples and the majestic mountains of the Boland were not the subjects that Schreuder preferred. The few times I saw him framing these couples, he seemed strained and distracted; what photos did reach the papers were nothing special. I followed him, stealthily, when he undertook his true photographic expeditions, and I was not satisfied until I saw him switch into what I called "Schreuder mode".

Suddenly, his movements would become supple and un-predictable, a flexible, swerving ritual of looking, pointing and shooting, as though, in the middle of the everyday routine, he was taking part in a parade of miracles. Always on the fringe of the procession, the festival, the meeting, he moved with his tripod camera, an ally with which he would fuse under a black cloth, becoming a two-headed, five-legged being clicking and flashing away, aiming the lens at a dripping gutter, a fallen handkerchief, a postbox in the column of shadow cast by a lamppost – as though these things were drenched in the light of revelation.

Would you not also have been curious about such a figure in a neat little bourgeois nest like Stellenbosch? My snooping could establish only two actual facts about him. His parents were music therapists at the School for the Blind in Worcester. He had a blind twin sister, so the story went, a singer with a beautiful soprano voice. Was this why he became a photographer, I wondered – to see twice? To compensate for his sister's disability?

Why did you not just ask him, you might wonder, and it is a fair question; everything could have been so different if I had taken the route of compassionate interest.

But I was cautious, ladies and gentlemen. I was only twenty-three years old and the man was outlandishly pale, with a roaming gaze, his complexion often tinged by melancholy. He was tall and thin, with a right shoulder that he carried just slightly too high. He had an irregular gait. On his right index finger, he wore a ring set with lapis lazuli – a talisman for pressing the shutter button. This was the kind of oddly ringed hobbling man against whom Protestant Church parents warned their decent daughters in those days. I had my own reasons for thinking he was an adversary. Remember, I was a freshly hatched philosophy student, kitted out for the first time with the analytical instruments of Marxism. In my mind, artistic affectation and related bourgeois phenomena could hardly be treated with sufficient suspicion.

It was therefore against my better judgement that, from time to time, I would strike up a conversation with Schreuder if I ran into him by accident, or pretended to run into him by accident. Out of guilt for spying on him, or pity because he was such a loner, I would begin with some excuse. It was never a smooth conversation. Schreuder had a stutter, you see. If he wanted to say something, he first had to take a deep breath and then spit out a few quick sentences, after which he would take a sesame-seed bar from his pocket and stuff a piece of it into his mouth. I had to stand un-nervingly close to him to hear what he was saying, and then listen to speculations I found both utterly fascinating and more or less useless: the function of medieval allegory, the structure of a fugue.

For a few days after one of these meetings, I would be slightly off kilter, partly because I knew there would soon be a gift from him, left on the front porch of my residence: a book about the Catholic suppression of the European Guild of Funerary Violinists in 1830, or the arrival of the first sparrow in South Africa in 1936 in the luggage of an English traveller. They were obscure second-hand books, full of closely written annotations in his hand. Sometimes there was a posy, carnations or stocks, a pot of honey in the comb. And always a card: Dear Miss Van Niekerk, thank you so much for the chat. And then, without any context or explanation, the title of a piece of music by Tallis or a reference to some detail of a painting: the crucified figure on the lute in *The Garden of Earthly Delights*. Often a poem by Emily Dickinson, written on the back of one of his photographs:

At half-past three a single bird
Unto a silent sky
Propounded but a single term
Of cautious melody.

At half-past four, experiment
Had subjugated test,
And lo! her silver principle
Supplanted all the rest.

At half-past seven, element
Nor implement was seen,
And place was where the presence was,
Circumference between.

I did not think much of these gifts at the time, ladies and gentle-men, and yet I never threw them away. I kept all the Schreuderiana in a special drawer. Later, the collection became a reference source in which I still find learning materials for my writing students, who are so utterly lacking in curiosity and so slow on the uptake in general.

(*Pause*) But I have realised that I was the one who was slow and had little insight, who was indifferent to these gestures of friendship (*unlock the box, lay it down flat*). Why, you might ask, was I so nonchalant?

I was studying hard, I was active in leftist student politics, I was under a lot of pressure as editor of the campus newspaper. I had no time for a dropout with a camera round his neck, was what I told myself. He had better understand that. It was not so much his age or occupation, but rather a feeling of asymmetry that made me, with my practical approach to things, feel somewhat uncomfortable around him. Fruit bat, I caught myself thinking, werewolf, sesame sower.

There was derisive laughter one day at a student festival where he was working when a sheaf of black-and-white photographs slipped from an envelope in his briefcase, falling under the feet of the dancers: a skirt blown up above the rear wheel of a bicycle, a gardenia under a bell jar, the hands of a young man tying a shoelace, a stone in a river, a book entitled *Huisvlyt* held to a girl's chest. Shadows of leaves on a whitewashed wall.

Ashamed of my fellow students' sneering, I helped him pick up the photographs and put them back in the envelope. I could not help but notice what was written on the front: "On the latticework of nothingness – 1975". And below it, an address in Minserie Street, where I knew he was lodging in a room at the home of old Mrs Gershater, one of the last Jewish inhabitants of Stellenbosch.

I caught his eye. They are beautiful pictures, Mr Schreuder, I said. Do you think I could come and see how you develop them?

He inhaled sharply, shoved a sesame bar in his mouth.

It took me a night to realise that "beautiful" was not the right word. The photos kept me up: half a girl on a bicycle, a faceless shoelacer, a conscientious headless virgin. A stone in the water, shadows on the wall, a flower behind glass. Trivialities. Why did they unsettle me?

Luckily, dear listeners, one's youthful ignorance prevents one from knowing exactly what one is getting oneself into, and what one can afford to rebel against (*look at the box*).

Not long after this sleepless night, I called on him at his place of residence in Minserie Street, despite my uneasiness. I did not know the number of the house, but when I caught an aroma of cloves at the last door on the street, I walked round the house, trod carefully through a bed of stocks in full bloom, and knocked on a side door. It took a while before it was opened. And there was Schreuder with his ruffled hair and his deep-set eyes, dressed in a threadbare dressing gown, the sleeves bunched up, revealing his veiny forearms. Disgusting dodo, I thought, gothic creep. But I steeled myself.

I was wondering if I could come see how you develop your photographs, I said, and when he blinked at the glare behind me, I added that this technique of developing photos seemed to me quite magical.

What is desire without technique, he said. I noticed his full lips, his dark hair curling wildly around his ears.

Desire for what? I asked. It slipped out before I could think.

C-come inside, he said, and I went straight in, stepping over the bed of flowers, over the doormat, over the threshold, into the odd-smelling music-filled twilight that was Schreuder's home. The floorboards gave slightly beneath my feet.

I spent the afternoon in an old-fashioned linen cupboard on legs that had been converted into a darkroom of sorts, a Bach violin solo coming from a cassette player in one corner. Bent over next to me with tongs, Schreuder lifted the sheets from the trays of solution and pinned them up on washing lines above our heads: a section of a lily, a knee beneath a pair of school shorts. Every second or third sheet was scrunched up and summarily stuffed into an overfull black bag. After a while he started indicating that I should hold something for him, pass him something, discard something, hang something; a ripple in a dam, a forehead over a washbasin, a key in a saucer, a half-opened book in a woman's lap. There, in the damp, swaying box, where neither of us said a word for a full two and a half hours, I turned into his accomplice. The closeness of our bodies in the rocking, creaking cupboard – it reminded me of an ark – the red light, the gestures, the violin, the sounds of submersion, the images looming up, the photos dripping around my shoulders in a glistening palpitating dimension, all suffocated and aroused me. Would I get out of there alive?

Once we were finished, to regain my composure, I lit a cigarette and took from my bag a copy of the campus paper and a bottle of St Augustine, my first gift to him. He glanced at the paper and opened the bottle. We drank the wine from tumblers, sitting opposite each other in two old armchairs.

Now, explain, I said, my voice as matter-of-fact as possible, the technique and the uhm . . . desire. He looked at me, but without meeting my gaze, his eyes searching, as though he wanted to cast a lasso over my head.

He drew a breath, looked away; I had to lean forward in my chair to hear him.

I want to catch things, no, not catch, release . . .

Liberate? I asked.

From their ou-ou-outlines, y-yes.

He spoke faster still between the deep breaths, so softly that I had to lean even further forward to hear him. I began to feel he wanted to devour me. Cannibal, I thought; but not for long, because the stutter was in Schreuder mode, it was rhythmic, like a piece of music.

With his photos, he wanted to *grab* things. Not as they *were*, but as they would *become*, through wind, through touch, through the lust of molecules. He wanted to catch them, but without injuring them, in chains of light and shadow, no, he wanted to catch them in their slipping away, he wanted to unleash *his* yearning upon *them*, furthermore, he wanted to *participate* in them, in *one* breath, in *one* light. He wanted to capture the forehead, the lily, the water, but not bound in skin or ripple or silhouette, he wanted to liberate the things, no, the ordinary *perception* of things, the *viewers* themselves, their *eyes*, his *own* eyes, from a state of enantiomorphism.

A state of what? I asked, but he did not hear me. He drank quickly. His face was so close to mine, I could feel his glow against my cheek.

He was a photographer of spasms and shimmers and metamorphoses, he said, he wanted to make visible the fuck-up and the fervour of fleeting moments. He believed in the shrrrr and drrr of things, and he wanted to capture their this-way-and-that and their vibration, their loose threads and insteps, their faulty frothing, did I get it? Their *fermentation*.

Cheers, I said, wondering if he was trying to seduce me. Our glasses were empty. He refilled them, took a packet of Sezamki from the pocket of his dressing gown and offered me some. Then he motioned with both hands, as though he was pushing a lever into a hole and carefully prying something out.

Crowbar? I guessed, with a mouth full of sweet sesame seed.

C-crowbar out, he said, the eyes of the b-bunker people who define things, a shoe a shoe, a mouth a mouth, a finch a finch, lexicographers, idolaters, indicating the h-here and there, all under the rule of U-u-ubu.

Ubu? I asked. The word hung in the air.

It was growing dark in Schreuder's back room; it was time for me to leave. Was that a smile on his face?

Look at the Progs, he went on. Sleepwalkers, just like the right-wing zombies in Cabinet.

He opened my paper on the floor. I had used photographs of the riots in Soweto with my leading articles. He went on, straight-faced. I could swear his ears were moving under those locks.

These photographers, he said, for them revolution is a manifesto clenched in a raised fist. And all the while the planet is boiling from the inside and there is a deluge of light about our ears. The revolution is just *one* swing of the pendulum, if only people would realise that, Schreuder said as he swung his long arms slowly before me. Was he trying to hypnotise me?

In turbulent times, one must photograph the m-m-moon, he sighed.

The scent of the stocks was drifting through the window. I got up. He looked at me. Politics is nothing but wallpaper, he said, and shoved the newspaper aside with a long foot and a sardonic snort.

Enough is enough, I cried, and there and then, ladies and gentlemen, I stiffened my spine and laid it on him, a full-on lecture, yes, I, arrogant child that I was, told the dreamy-eyed Schreuder: There's no place for your sort in our country, Peter. Wake up, this is Africa, South Africa. Nobody gives a shit about releasing finches from their outlines in this country. Out here, liberation is concerned with the oppressed masses in an undemocratic system. You have at your disposal the skills to help mobilise the world for the struggle, but you waste your time on lilies and ripples! At least make some useful pictures; put your work in service of something greater than yourself.

Then I stuck out my hand and said, thank you for what you've told me about development, now please spend some time developing your social responsibility.

He looked away, his head held high. He got up and opened the door for me.

I went home and looked up "enantiomorph". A term from mineralogy for two crystals forming each other's mirror image. I put the book back on the shelf. Enantiomorphism, shmenantiomorphism, I thought. Stay away from the man, Van Niekerk, he's bad news.

Two weeks later, I got an invitation from Schreuder to join him for a music recital in Worcester at the School for the Blind. He included the programme. Duets from the cantatas of Bach, performed by Philip Schreuder Senior, contra tenor, and Elizabeth Schreuder, soprano. Father and daughter. I was surprised at the warm tone of the invitation, as though nothing had happened: I hope you will come with me. Best, the finch redeemer.

Oh, go finch yourself, I thought, with your blind Bach and your singing sister, the Von Trapps of the Hex River Valley, no doubt. I never responded to the invitation.

Shortly afterwards, a cassette tape was delivered to my residence, with the usual postcard accompanying it: Dear Van, pity you could not come. It was an exceptional performance. Here is a recording for you. I am going to seek my fortune in Johannesburg. I cannot stand this town another moment. Thank you for your interest in my work, it means more to me than you might realise. I shall stay in touch. Your friend, Peter.

I did not appreciate him calling me "Van" all of a sudden. This was my nickname in struggle circles. I shoved the cassette into a box of Schreuder knick-knacks. "Friend", I thought, you and I are from different planets. May you find your fortune threefold.

To find mine, I went to the University of Amsterdam to study philosophy. I soon forgot Peter Schreuder and his impossible desires. Every day, in the Netherlands of the nineteen-eighties, I got confirmation for my idea that it was the artist's responsibility to instrumentalise his art in the service of social justice agendas. I was especially impressed by a demonstration of Dutch literary theorists, complete with rattles and pot lids, in front of Athenaeum on the day VS Naipaul came to Amsterdam for a book signing. This is how intellectuals should emerge from their ivory towers, I wrote home.

It was during this period of study, on a visit back home in 1982, that I saw Schreuder's first retrospective exhibition. *Mirror of South Africa*. The title was a play on the propaganda film *Spieël van Suid-Afrika*, which was shown as an opener in all bioscopes in the sixties: army platoons and ministers' wives with ornate hats at the opening of parliament. Schreuder held up a different mirror. His earlier pictures, the cyclist, the shoelace tier, the home economics student, were blocked in a group against one wall like half of a diptych. Against the opposite wall, there were detail shots from the parallel world of black people: the dress and the bicycle, the hands and the shoe, the exercise book held against a black girl's chest. The contradictions spoke louder than any eighties leftist journo's rapportage: the rusty bicycle rim, the worn shoe heel, the faded dress. Schreuder saw everything: politicians stiff and bloated in their lordship, white proletarians against a backdrop of car wrecks and old refrigerators, migrant labourers waiting under blankets on apartheid train platforms, black men naked under the measuring sticks of mine doctors, township children naked among dogs and porridge pots, white schoolboys in school uniforms locked in a brotherhood of fear and superiority.

All the typical Schreuder qualities were there, the annunciatory light, the unexpected angle, the focus on detail, but these aestheticising technicalities could now be ignored. The gardenia in the jar, the stone and the moon, bless them, no longer formed part of the ensemble, and oblivion itself no longer starred in this particular play. Here were the current political developments in South Africa in rich, truly meaningful images. The Afrikaner Nationalist government media called Schreuder a traitor. The African National Congress, on the other hand, absolved him from the cultural boycott and he was free to exhibit his work in Europe. I wrote a letter of congratulation and delivered it to the gallery. My stupid rashness of ten years ago at least served to mobilise your talent towards a good cause, I wrote.

Humility, as you can see, has never really been one of my strong points. As a postscript, I added that he should come over to my place for a glass of St Augustine when I returned to South Africa the following year. I added my address in Onderpapegaaiberg, and both my phone numbers. I ought to have looked at the moon before I wrote them down.

But I did not, I was blinded by the light of the sun dog. Peter Schreuder was under control, I thought, or at least I was in control of the effect he had on me, or inside me. Was it during this time that I happened to read in the paper that his parents and sister had been killed in a car accident? A photo taken at the funeral: Schreuder, with his palms stretched out to the open grave as though he was handing something over, or accepting something. Did I send a card? I cannot remember.

In the nineties, during the liberalisation of the country, Schreuder documented the development of the informal economy in an exhibition entitled *Mobile Contractors*. All along highways one saw adverts for the new entrepreneurs, written in twisted letters on a piece of plywood or cardboard and tied to a lamppost or propped up by rocks. *Simon Mhlobe, Painter. Cut throat price, I do not mess*, with a Vodacom number. *Easyboy Manto, private contractor for your dirty jobs big and small*, an MTN number written in yellow chalk. Schreuder phoned these numbers and went to photograph these small-business owners in their shabby clothes, painting living rooms and tiling kitchen floors in up-market white homes.

I told my writing students about the project: This is how you should do it, I said, you are the documenters, the witnesses, the conscience, everything else is egotistical and a waste of time.

1994 to 2004, the decade of the New South Africa's entry into the global economy, coincided with Schreuder's international success, including here in the Netherlands. He won prize after prize and his earlier work was republished. Glossy magazines like *The New Statesman* printed his portraits of the new South African rulers and the black economically empowered elite. Although he always sent me a postcard when I published a new novel and phoned me on my birthday, I never thought I would see him again. I had assumed that he would settle somewhere overseas, like many successful South African artists. The multi-cultural societies of Europe had more than enough problems to allow a critical photographer to carve out a new niche for himself.

But then late one evening in the summer of 2006, there was a knock on my door and there stood Schreuder, with his high right shoulder in a khaki safari jacket and his camera around his neck. He stuck his hand through the security gate, not in greeting but in a different, more urgent gesture.

I have a bit of a situation, he said, and nodded in the direction of an SUV parked outside.

I was aghast.

You're the only person here who can help me, he said.

I tried to look past him, to see who was in the car. Two people. One got out, a black guy in a security uniform. He took a big suitcase and two smaller ones from the boot.

My bodyguard, he said, and motioned for the man to come closer. Marshall Ngcuka, he introduced himself. A big fellow in a bulletproof vest, boots, revolver at his hip.

Marshall accidentally shot someone who tried to steal my mobile phone. A ricochet, right in the calf, flesh wound. And I got bitten too.

He reached out again. His palm was blue and swollen, with two holes below the knuckles.

Human-animal bite, he grimaced. I wouldn't let go of the phone. The thief is in the Jeep. He's bleeding, but I don't want trouble with hospitals and police. Can we stay with you for a few days? Please?

What else could I do, ladies and gentlemen? Schreuder was at my door, white as a sheet. He looked as though he might collapse at any moment. Behind him, the bodyguard was supporting a young black boy, leaving a trail of blood on the pathway.

You can have the garage and the outside toilet, I said, but you'll have to sleep on the floor.

Getting the story out of them was like pulling teeth. I gave them all sweet tea, whisky and paracetamol, and sat with them at my kitchen table. The photographer, the bodyguard and the pickpocket. As far as I could gather, the accident had occurred in Khayelitsha, where Schreuder was taking photographs for his new project: portraits of criminals out on parole among their own people, victims included, in the very street or room where the crime had been committed.

I looked at the faces around my table. Schreuder was slouched and ashen, the bodyguard was much too big for my kitchen chair, the thief was a boy of barely sixteen.

Schreuder was breathing heavily. The deal with the boy, Mandla, was that his wound would be nursed, he would get a bed and meals until he was better, clothes and a pair of shoes to take home, and payment of thirty rands an hour for six hours per day.

Payment for what? I asked.

Marshall snorted.

For sitting, said Schreuder, with a searching gaze directed at the boy's face.

Sitting? I asked.

For photographs, said Schreuder, for portraits, for close-ups of my personal robber. As a part of my forthcoming exhibition *On Parole*.

My leg is sore, said Mandla.

First, I had my vet come around, a small-town swindler who would do anything if the price was right. Schreuder got a tetanus shot and some ARVs, the phone thief got painkillers and a bandage for his wound, and the bodyguard some pills for his insomnia. For the next two weeks, I played hostess to my three visitors. I stood in the kitchen peeling onions, my mouth full of water, thinking so much for l'art engagé.

The garage was Schreuder's laboratory. A darkroom was no longer needed, since he developed most of his photographs digitally nowadays, on a laptop. But there was darkness all around. The garage was in chaos, a dangerous quarantine ward with a four-headed occupancy: the shooter, the casualty, the photographer and me, the ever-serving, if reluctant, Martha.

Schreuder photographed every single movement his assailant made. In the overcrowded burrow between two washing lines, beside a gurgling gas lamp, he zig-zagged around the prisoner. Marshall smacked Mandla when the boy took one of his cigarettes without asking. Schreuder took pictures. The vet came to bandage Mandla's wound. Schreuder took pictures. Mandla leaned on a crutch as he urinated in the outside toilet. Schreuder took pictures, endlessly. You are mine, I heard him say to the boy, I watch over your comings and goings, I shall capture every stirring of your soul, every plan that dawns within you. Mandla protested, this was not how he had understood the deal. Peter and Marshall fought about taking turns to guard the boy, everyone slept too much or too little, the roof had sprung a leak in the winter storms. Through it all, Schreuder held long, tense sessions in my living room with Tony Morton, the reproduction technician working on the coming exhibition. My entire house was hung with proofs for *On Parole*, a mob of criminal faces on the walls, on the bookshelves and on the drawn curtains. Meanwhile, Schreuder taunted me, ever more incomprehensible, stuttering more than usual, his eyes closed for long periods, pretending they needed rest. To see the world as a dog or a goose sees it, he said, would be liberation for every photographer. No more human confusion, only a wondrous enlightenment.

After two weeks, I had had enough. The neighbours were starting to complain about the shouting matches in my yard. I told Marshall to clean up my garage and to take the boy back to the township. I found Schreuder a hotel in Cape Town, close to the gallery where his exhibition was to open. I held out my hand, demanding the keys to my garage.

This was not the end of the catastrophe. On the opening night of *On Parole*, one of the gang members Schreuder had photographed in Mitchells Plain showed up at the gallery with his lawyer, demanding a massive sum of money as compensation for libel. The exhibition itself was not received well. The headlines were damning: "Racism and stereotyping in Schreuder's new work" and "Peter Schreuder disgraced". The most painful blow came from the magazine *Art South Africa*, from the pen of his photographer colleague Jonathan Silberfuss: "Shameless pictorial exploitation of the subaltern – Schreuder regresses to the cliché of the highway robber".

Two days after the opening, Schreuder was back on my porch. Someone had slashed the Jeep's tyres in the street outside the gallery. He was so upset, I had no choice but to invite him in. I gave him a sedative and a hot-water bottle and put him to bed, then went to my study to consider my options.

Or rather, to consider *his* options.

His options as a photographer, you see?

For this was the question: What subject matter could my friend direct his attention to after this scandal, with any hope of retaining his professional integrity? I would suggest a subject as far away from the political as possible. I did not want to be in the company of this albatross from my youth for a moment longer. I would take him straight to the airport the following morning and put him on a plane to the famous uMkhuze wild bird reserve, where numerous rare and threatened species could still be seen. I had booked him into a luxurious lodge and paid for a month upfront.

What more could I do for his salvation? While he slept, I visited websites on bird behaviour and prepared an envelope of printouts, obscure information that I thought might be of interest to him.

In the car on the way to the airport, I lectured him for a second time. With my eyes fixed on the road and my voice smoothly inspiring, I said: You are old, you are tired. You are the most important photographer of your generation. You have taken great artistic and personal risks, you've reached the highest rung in your work. But you have to know when to step back. It is time to rest; not to stop working, but to scale back, with no loss of meaning or significance. Think of it this way: Humans are destroying the planet. There aren't enough photographers of your calibre working in nature photography. Rest your eyes, take your time, the narina trogon is waiting for you, the great blue heron, the lilac-breasted roller, the fork-tailed drongo. We may very well be the last people to see them in the wild.

Could I make him change course? He just stared abstractedly into space. Was this what petit mal looked like?

Oh, come on, don't look so woeful, I said, it's not a death sentence. Regimes come and regimes go, the despots will always be with us, as will the poor, the jealous critics and the stupid journalists – but not the birds. Take photographs for bird calendars. Go hand them out at schools in poor areas, give them a talk on green issues. Let the WWF sponsor you; you won't have trouble getting a subsidy with your reputation. And you'll be doing something for your country in your twilight years. Limit the scope, it's time for introspection. Split the lark, I said, quoting his own beloved Emily Dickinson: Split the lark, and you'll find the music.

By the way, and now there was a seductive turn in my voice, have you ever seen a lark mirror?

I deliberately did not look at him, but I felt his gaze on me, his first reaction since being bullied into going to the airport. From the corner of my eye, I could see that he had never heard of such a thing.

Bingo! I thought, for the first time in my life *I* have made *you* curious.

I got him to open the envelope containing printouts of articles I had found on the website of one Herman Arentsen from Volendam, the author of the only book about the history and construction of the lark mirror[iv].

Something to read in your treehouse in uMkhuze, I said.

With this reading matter, his e-ticket and a bottle of St Augustine, I left him in the drop-off zone.

A clean break, I thought as I drove home.

(Pause)

I'm getting ahead of the story, ladies and gentlemen, but do any of you know what a lark mirror is?

(Pause)

Shall I show you?

(In complete silence, the components are fitted together and the lark mirror is set up, carefully, so that it doesn't start spinning. Then continue with a cautious poker face.)

What you see here, ladies and gentlemen, is a traditional lure used when hunting birds, in widespread use since the seventeenth century in southern Europe and in England[v]. Those of you who become unwell as a result of spinning spokes and lanes of trees striped with shadows should perhaps close your eyes and just listen to the rest of my story.

Schreuder stayed away much longer than the month I had booked for him at the reserve. Half a year later he was back at my door, this time with feverish eyes and a B3-sized cardboard file full of photographs. Not exactly the picture of a photographer back from safari. I was wary of a second occupation of my garage. I'm heading overseas, I lied, and tenants are coming to stay here.

Excellent, he said, then the photos won't be in your way,

they're nothing anyway, I just wanted to drop them off, if I may. I've sold my place, I can no longer stand this continent, I'm also leaving.

Schreuder said goodbye and drove off without looking back at me where I stood on my front porch with the file in my arms. I did not look at the contents, just stuffed it into a cupboard full of many years' worth of his miscellaneous detritus, irritated by the door that would not stay shut. I would have to unpack and sort out the entire Schreuder smorgasbord. Why did I have such an eerie sense of premonition? Was it the result of touching all the unacknowledged gifts? It was not long before I received Schreuder's first epistle from Europe – a densely inscribed airmail letter from Amsterdam.

Dear M.

I am tracking a drifter who sleeps in the snow behind my apartment every night. He thinks I am taking photographs of him, but my camera is aimed at the sky. He drops me little indecipherable notes in the street and I follow him every day to the antique shop on the Spiegelgracht, where he spends hours staring at something in the display. Today I went closer for the first time to see what in god's name it could be – would you believe it! A lark mirror. I recognised it from those printouts you gave me before sending me off on the famous "bird-cure" you had dreamt up. I bought it immediately, a Robillard from 1890, mounted in a wooden box lined with felt. The shopkeeper relayed the rather tall tale that Charcot had hypnotised an entire hall full of people with a similar apparatus. In France, he said, miroir aux alouettes still refers to a politician who misleads the people with false promises.

I have turned the luring-glass into my coat of arms. After all, is not seducing the viewer with false images exactly what I do?

By the way, have you looked at the file with bird photographs I left you? In them, I illustrate my latest insight, or my oldest, more radically than ever before.

Anyway, the crocuses are in full flower in the parks, I must go and try out the alwetierra. That is Maltese for lark mirror. I shall let you know if it works!

I hope to hear back from you.

Your ally,

Mr Meltwater

I reread the letter. Why did he so blindly exaggerate my every suggestion, going so far beyond my obvious intention? Why, in fact, did he submit with such heart and soul to my directives, only to overdo them so grossly? A shrill pigeon cooed in the garden. I put the letter in the cupboard, on top of the file, and attacked the spinach patch in my yard with a shovel to work out my frustration.

The next missive arrived a month later, a postcard this time.

Ahoy, Van

"Dis heerlike lente, die winter's verby", and I am sitting in a meadow near Oudekerk. My cameras have taken a dip in the Vecht, my aerial shots of the snow sleeper have been posted to the city archives. Herr Gott sei Dank, my final crime. But the Robillard, oh how the Robillard works! Not just for larks either, most of the smaller fowl fall for it. They drop from the air, remain paralysed for a few minutes, and I keep them warm in my lap until they come to and fly away. Best of all, I also fall for the bloody thing. Pallaksch! Sometimes for half an hour or more. And then I wake as I used to be before I became someone. Smooth and solid, shallow keeled, on the endless river of my youth, a small ship raising its white sails. How is Peng there in Onderpapegaaiberg? Will you never write back?

Your sidekick

Scardinelli

Peng? Scardinelli? Speleologist, I thought. Postcard in hand, I stood by the window, looking out at my garden. It was the month of May. The air was restless. A small shower of little yellow leaves from the syringa. Could it be that Schreuder was trying to teach me something? But who cares so much about a friend that he would take so many risks with his own work, with his very life, for this purpose? I sat down to write him a letter, but it kept digressing into admonishments and self-justification, and that was not what I wanted to say.

A month after the postcard, I got an overseas call from the Immigratie- en Naturalisatiedienst. Officer Johan Moens was formal: Yes, he was calling with regard to one Peter Schreuder, well known as a photographer in the Netherlands, who had given him my name. Schreuder had been found in a confused state on a country lane outside Amsterdam, and taken to a shelter for illegal foreigners to be medically stabilised. His visa had expired two weeks earlier, and he was being deported by means of a special travel concession, along with his belongings, including a number of water-damaged cameras and a wooden box containing a device for attracting birds. Here is the flight number and arrival time, I could pick him up at the airport in Cape Town the following morning, an official from the South African Department of Home Affairs and a delegate from the Dutch consulate would be there with the papers I had to sign to acknowledge receipt of one VO-NDEL, A/O-3: adult foundling, non-delinquent, illegal, a foreigner, dependent and doli incapax grade 3. If I had any objections, he advised that I get legal counsel.

What's wrong with him? I asked. You will find the psychiatric evaluation in the inner pocket of the deported individual's jacket, said Moens. Did Schreuder smile at the airport when I reached into his jacket to retrieve the envelope, warm from his body heat, crumpled after the long journey? It felt like the bread cast upon the waters that was found after many days.

I had known he was epileptic. The doctors who had examined him also suspected multiple personality disorder. The recommendation in the report was that he be nursed in a stable environment, with some Seroquel handy in case he caused trouble.

But there is nothing multiple about Schreuder, ladies and gentlemen, he is singular, a blank slate, and he is no trouble at all. He moves without knowing where he is going, sits without knowing where he is sitting; he is calm and composed, just going with the flow. A big grey-haired child in my back garden with his face aimed at the heavens, breathing calmly. His body is dried-out wood, his heart cooled ash, a smile without a face. The specialists cannot find any neurological problems. A freak mental standstill, they call it. He is as he is, but he is gone. He will not open his mouth. He refuses. He closes his eyes, as though he is afraid he himself might leak from his sockets.

Well, now I am the leak. I have come here and told the whole story. I left him with a nurse and a domestic worker, without his toy.

(Look at the lark mirror.) Since fetching Schreuder at the airport, I have been holding on to this *(touch the lark mirror)*. He would spin it ceaselessly, and at night it had to go to bed with him. I fixed the head with a clamp to prevent further damage; a dazed man was bad enough, I did not have the strength for a yardful of paralysed birds as well. But why the fixation? Was it a kind of transitional object, like a toddler's blankie, something taking the place of the original object? But what transition was at play here, and what loss?

If there was an answer, I started to think, it would be found in his work.

For the past two years, before tucking him in for the night, I have often sat next to him on his bed and paged through his photo books with him. I put his hands on the glossy pages. Here is your work, I would say, look at what you have accomplished: your fatherland, as nobody had seen it before you. But the doors stayed firmly shut. I was the one who had to open up. I brought out the letters, postcards, photos, dried stocks, a small jar of crystallised honey, an audio tape: a little museum of friendship which I curated, there in his back room. In the morning when I took him coffee in bed, I dusted everything off and put the items in his hands one by one, read him the words he once wrote to me and secretly watched his face for any kind of sign, but I never got more than a smile. I had to go and look at myself in the mirror.

A month ago, I took the big B3 file from his long-ago bird safari in Natal from the cupboard for the first time. Had I really thought it would be filled with perfectly framed, high-resolution colour shots of sunbirds? I put on some violin music for the occasion and, sitting next to Schreuder on the side of his bed, I opened the cover.

Twigs, leaves, rocks. Everything in grayscale, empty and bare. Where are the birds, Schreuder? I asked. Did he want to say something? I saw something glistening between his eyelids. I paged back and started over, and then I saw it: the forked branch of a bushwillow, prepared for a parrot, seven grooves in the sandstone to accommodate the raven, a strelitzia with its blue and orange petals, erect for the sugarbird. There were chimneys and telephone poles rigid with anticipation, and reeds and grass rustling from departure: an essay on absence, full of gusts and slipstreams and the play of enlivened light.

I stood before Schreuder and took his hands in mine. They were light and dry. Where did the sigh come from, from me or from him? Will he still be alive when I return? Do I still have time to process what I began to grasp in that moment? Rich material. The cure of the birds, the shirr and the drrr, taking part in the great escape, in a single breath, in singular light, the release of all things from their outlines, the negative way. How could I have been so stupid? Rubbing his nose in my liberation politics and my nature conservation as though they were the only valuable agendas? Maybe that was when I decided I had to tell the whole sad saga to somebody one day.

I had helped to make his career, but I am afraid I almost destroyed his life. I feel regret. Not that he would want that. There is also something to celebrate, he might have said, insofar as one can be walking the plank, celebrating the approach of the edge and feeling, more importantly, a kind of vulnerability, one's powerlessness before the overwhelming being-there of it all.

Maybe that is what he would have said, and not in such a stupidly emphatic way either. He would have stuttered it out in Schreuderian, that untethered Orphean language of his. And I would have had to extract my lesson from it, teachings of the mysterious surfaces of things, the fathomlessness of existence for which not only the photographer but also the writer ultimately bears responsibility. But would that be the whole story? I think not. The precipice was much closer, the abyss was me, my endless inability to be his comrade, to have a bond with a giving, trusting soul. Is this how I missed my chance? I do not know, I am trying to make up for it.

The sons of the domestic worker and the nurse helped me to lay out a garden for him. Stocks, carnations, a beehive, a small orchard of lemon trees behind the house. Now in early summer the garden, to quote the bard, ist wie ein Kind, das Gedichte weiß, fragrant with blossoms and honey. Every morning I take him to his seat under the fig tree. He does not eat or drink much, not even a sesame bar. The sparrows peck at the seeds between his feet. His vacant smiling face sets the tone for the household. We do our work around him: We read to him, we garden, we clean the house, do shopping. Because of his silence in our midst, we do not talk much either. Sometimes one of the young men catches me when I am just sitting with my eyes closed, trying to write a poem, listening to the rumbling on the roads all around, to the clicking and bubbling of my own insides, the often audible buzz of the cosmos. Come on then, they say, back to work, for the night cometh.

When the robin starts singing in the twilight, and I hear Schreuder answering outside, his head tilted back, his lips pouted to whistle, I go and stand by his chair and drone out an accompaniment. The bird, the augur and the dimwit. A caller, a respondent and a witness. In the upper register, the clear, soaring crepuscular birdsong, then a whistled response in a fainter human timbre, and right at the bottom, a late, dumbfounded bass pedal. It is a fragile refrain filled with variation: "Ein Hauch um nichts. Ein Wehn im Gott. Ein Wind."

In those moments, I think back to the concert of Bach cantatas in Worcester that Schreuder invited me to more than thirty years ago, to meet his family. I imagine our evening hymn in the garden as an echo of the duets sung by his father and his blind sister.

I have brought along the recording of that performance at the School for the Blind in Worcester, dear listeners, an exceptional recording indeed, and one I often listen to with the last remaining family member, now that all the performers have passed on, the daughter, the father, the mother on bass. The deceased who sustain the earth. Only in this double world can their voices become eternal and generous. In closing, let me play you a fragment.

(Play the music from the cantata "Wer da glaubet und getauft wird", the choral (duet), "Herr Gott Vater, mein starker Held". Set the lark mirror spinning, once right, once left, right again, let it go, spin it again, until the last bar. Stop it when the singing ends, put it back in the box and close the lid at the exact moment the final chord of the accompaniment is played.)

Endnotes

i   The word comes from the Latin *inaugurare*, meaning to confirm some-
    one in a position ceremonially based on a reading of signs. An augur is
    a bone thrower and a diviner who predicts the future, someone who can
    determine destiny by looking at signs: clouds or the flight of birds, the
    livers of animals or the yolks of eggs, or bones and droppings and teeth.
    Therefore, an inaugural lecture may be described as soothsaying based
    on premonitions.

ii *Oggend van 'n waterfiskaal*

    Allagot! geglip uit die knukkels
    van hierdie kant se koskans- en hansmaker,
    wip die waterfiskaal die oggendkier in,
    kaneeeeeel van verbasing op sy bors,
    onder sy kruidnagelkloutjies die rinkink-rulle
    spiksplinterspuwende Dwarsriviersand,
    tinktuuuuur van manelkwik geveer op sy flanke,
    strak in die frak die keil platgekam
    akkelief hy oor die akkers tot die waterkant, kyk!
    triljarrrrrrrrrrde klein en groot fiskale innie spiekspiegel –
    hokaai kohorte kansvatters –
    wat hy konter met pronkstand akimbo,
    knipstert na die kindlig in die oewerkrui,
    en wegstaan, kykso, eeeeene ollewagen onderbaadjie,
    hy is die slim en innigste godontglipper
    hier in die prilwilde hoogmakerson,
    !tewiek in sy keel sit sy roepnaam !tewiek
    soos 'n klok in die bergkut ketoooools
    van die mondsagte môre.

iii This lecture was originally presented in Leiden on 15 October 2009 as the Albert Verwey memorial lecture. In the Catholic holy calendar, 15 October is the festival of Saint Teresa, and on the ornithological calendar it is a day in the middle of the lark migration. "A Santa Teresa, allodole a distesa", say the Italian hunters: On Santa Teresa we see endless larks; on Malta it goes like this: "Il-kewba ta' Santa Tereza, ggib maghhal-alwett, l-ekri u ghasafar ohra tal ghana", which means: The star of Saint Teresa brings larks and siskins and other songbirds. Arentsen and Fenech, 2004: 26-27.

iv Arentsen, HF and Fenech, N. 2004. *Lark Mirrors: Folk Art from the Past*. Published by the authors.

v The lark mirror has been in use since the third century BC to lure birds to nets or towards shooters and has been employed in hunting small fowl in Malta until recently, albeit illegally so. It consists of a small wooden slat inlaid with mirrors. This is mounted to a metal shaft that spins smoothly in a wooden peg that is hammered into the ground. The slat is brought into motion using a clockwork mechanism or a string. Birds fly towards it in great numbers and fall from the air, as though hypnotised, and are then easily shot or trapped. Many reasons are given why larks would find these spinning mirrors attractive; they could think that it is water, or the sun, or a different flock of larks, or a new earth and a new heaven. Arentsen and Fenech, 2004: 21-25. See for example https://en.expertissim.com/lark-mirror-decoy-early-20th-century-12196827.

Acknowledgements

Lines and fragments from the work of the following poets have been included in the text, with or without direct references: Joseph von Eichendorff, Emily Dickinson, Jalāl ad-Dīn Muhammad Rumi, Rainer Maria Rilke, Louis MacNeice, Albert Verwey, TS Eliot, RL Stevenson, Paul van Ostaijen and Paul Celan. "The Percussionist" also includes a fragment from the fifteenth-century Maltese text "Il Cantilena" by Pietro Caxaro.

Thank you to the following individuals who read these stories during the writing process and who gave invaluable comments: Henda Strydom, Ena Jansen, Louise Viljoen, Hettie Scholtz, Alida Potgieter, Madri Victor, Rosemarie Buikema and the Naudé family. Thank you to Annette Portegies from Querido Publishers for her advice and support throughout the particular trajectory of the publication of the Dutch edition of the book, Marius Swart for the English translation, and to Henrietta Rose-Innes for her contribution to the English edition. Thank you also to Herman Arentsen for the information on lark mirrors. The inaugural lecture "The Swan Whisperer", presented on 12 August 2008, is included here with the kind permission of the University of Stellenbosch.

The Snow Sleeper

MARLENE VAN NIEKERK

The Snow Sleeper

MARLENE VAN NIEKERK

Printed in Australia
AUHW012056040219
308258AU00001B/1

9 780798 179256